Walker's Mission

WALKER'S MISSION

Don Hepler

HEPLER

AVALON BOOKS
THOMAS BOUREGY AND COMPANY, INC.
401 LAFAYETTE STREET
NEW YORK, NEW YORK 10003

PRINTED IN THE UNITED STATES OF AMERICA
ON ACID-FREE PAPER
BY HADDON CRAFTSMEN, SCRANTON, PENNSYLVANIA

Walker's Mission

Chapter One

It was good land, rich and green with tall waving grass except in the corral, where the horses had eaten everything down to the dirt. There was always a team in there too. Eight of the stupidest animals God ever put on this earth, they were waiting their turn to get hooked up and haul the stage farther west or east.

You'd hear the trumpet first, blowing loud, the notes telling everyone who was driving that particular stage. For example, Robin would blow three of the longest and clearest notes you ever heard, from down the scale to as high as he could get. Hear those notes and you always knew that Robin was coming with his big grin and friendly ways.

1

On the other hand, there were the short trills favored by Jess Wright. It always surprised me how such a quiet and slow man like Jess would pick fast trills for his horn, but that sound was his, and once heard it would never be forgotten by anybody.

No matter who was driving, the stage would come in and the people would get down and stomp out back to the necessary. Two of them out there. One for men and the other for women. Only there weren't too many women who rode the stage through here, so most of the time men used them both. Mighty rough trip, especially for women.

As for myself, I came in on that stage too, only I got off there and somehow never had a mind to get back on. I know it was the woman who made me stay. Just proves there's no fool like a romantic fool. Not that I got any romantic feelings toward her. I'm not that big a fool, least not yet. Just that I like to watch her. Like to watch her cope with the problems and the trying things that happen around here. Like to look at her face all smooth and sun-brown. Like to look at her eyes, kind of blue-green, and so clear it's like you can see right into her head. I like to watch her move, natural and easy, like weeds waving in the summer breeze.

Got no idea how she got here. Never asked and she never said. But I came on the stage and I got off and I never left yet.

I just started helping her out some, and she kept feeding me, and now it's like I belong here and this place is partly my responsibility too. Only it's not. Not really. I just came in on the stage and I got off and I never got back on. Yet.

My bum leg bothers me once in a while, but there's nothing wrong with my eyes or my back, so I can put in a day's work same as any other man. I'm twenty-four, I think, and a long ways from dead. She never asked me about my leg so I never told her. Never asked me about my gun, either. Why I wear it all the time, I mean. Actually, we don't talk much. But I think she must like me some, else why would she feed me and put up with me for all this time?

Now I got to replace the rail next to the gate where that stupid bay tried to jump out. Horses are the most stupid critters God ever put on this earth. 'Cept maybe men.

That horse must've thought he was one of those fancy Tennessee studs or something, 'cause he tried to jump a three-rail fence. Made an awful lot of noise, what with him squealin' and carryin' on, but I finally got him calmed down nice and proper.

I felt sorry for him actually, on account of he just wanted to get at that fancy mare the dude was riding. Sometimes I know just how he feels. That woman sure does have pretty eyes.

The guy dressed like a dude, but I could tell from the way he handled that mare when she got all nervous that he could handle a horse. Makes me interested in him, really. Man who can handle a horse like that can usually handle himself all around. He must be dressed like that so he can fool people. Don't know why. But he bears watching.

He shined right up to Sarah, all teeth and smiles and polish. Of course, she's nice right back, and I believe he thinks she shines on him too. Only, Sarah is nice to all people. Even me. So he's wasting his time.

I finish dropping the new rail in place, and I see her come out the door and shade her eyes as she looks in my direction. She starts on over to me, and I just stand there and watch her come. Fine lookin' woman. Just watchin' her move makes a man proud, if you know what I mean.

"You got it fixed," she says, and sounds pleased.

"Yes'm."

Funny how hard it is to talk to her. I mean, I got all this stuff going around in my mind, only nothing comes out.

She looks up at me, and the red afternoon sun makes her squint so she puts her hand up to shade her eyes. I can't help it if I'm tall and she has to look up to me. She looks me right in the eye with that steady calm look she has. "Supper's ready," she says. "Time to get washed up."

I follow her over to the house. Kind of makes me feel warm and soft inside when she walks beside me. She only comes up to my shoulder, and can't weigh more'n a hundred pounds, but she can make me sort of weaken up all over. I tried to imagine what it would be like to give her a hug one time when she was walking next to me. Tried real hard, and could almost feel her all soft and warm, reaching up to put her arms around me right back. But it just was too powerful, and so I sort of pushed it back and never tried to imagine it again.

The washbasin is around in back, of course, and she goes inside while I go around.

The dude is there ahead of me, and so's the Mexican and the kid who both came in on the stage. Might've known that anybody who looked like the dude would get to the wash water first. While we're waiting for the dude to finish, the Mexican, the kid, and I size each other up.

The Mexican shows the eye wrinkles of a man who's been squinting into many horizons. He's hard to age, but maybe he'd be thirty. Those thirty years were tough ones, though. Shows in his wiry build and see-all eyes. His clothes are dusty but his gun is clean, and he strikes me as a good man to have on my side in a fight. Better that than the other way around. He nods slightly in my direction and I nod back.

The other fellow is young. That doesn't necessarily mean stupid, especially in anyone with a little Indian in him, but he looks wild and dangerous. Like he doesn't think anything can ever happen to him. He'll learn, of course. If he lives, that is. He wears a cross-draw gun on his left side. Prob'ly itching to use it too.

The dude takes the towel down from the nail and the Mexican moves to the basin. He wets his hands and rubs the big yellow bar of lye soap between them. The kid turns to me.

"That woman yours?" he asks softly. The dude looks up, suddenly interested.

"I been lookin' out for her," I answer. I don't much like the question.

He laughs and says, "That means same as no, don't it?"

He doesn't really expect an answer so I don't give one. Meanwhile, I watch the Mexican work some lather out of the soap. About half of the small finger on his right hand is missing.

"She's a mighty lot of woman for you, kid," he says as he splashes in the basin.

The kid snorts. "Mighty lot?" he asks. "She don't even reach my shoulders."

The dude studies him for a second. "More than one way to be mighty," he says. He interests me. Educated, most likely, but from the way he talks, he just might be smart too. Big difference, you know.

I can see the kid thinking that over, worrying it around in his mind, trying to get all the meaning out of it. Not a bad sign in a kid.

I wash last and follow them into the dining room.

I always sit at the corner table, a habit I got into after Pa explained why it was a good idea. Got so I now feel something like a draft on my back if I don't have a wall running up by each shoulder. Seems like Sarah knows that, 'cause she always sets my place there in the corner even though it means she has to walk a little farther.

I always sort of wish she would sit and eat with me, only she never does. She eats in the kitchen, prob'ly where *she* feels safest. 'Course, if she did sit and eat with me, I'd prob'ly starve to death. Don't have any of those fancy manners, and I'd be so afraid of disgusting her that I prob'ly wouldn't eat anything at all.

Don't get me wrong. Ma taught us how to eat decent, and I don't spit and I chew with my mouth closed. But eating decent and fancy manners are two different things, I guess.

I go around the table to my chair and ease down. I take the thong off the hammer of my pistol, which is just something I do, like sitting in the corner.

I see the dude looking at me. He saw me unhook my pistol and he raises an eyebrow in question. I shrug slightly and his eyes crinkle a little in what must pass for a smile on him. He turns back to his plate, not looking at anybody in particular. Trying to be invisible. Good idea. If a man doesn't look anybody right in the eye, they'll generally leave him alone. The dude strikes me as a man who wants to be left alone, sittin' all by himself like that.

The Mexican and the kid are sitting together, only they aren't talkin' to each other at all. Just waiting for their food like the rest of us.

The Mexican has his back to the wall too. Guess I'm not the only careful man in the place.

Sarah brings in the food on big metal plates almost like pie pans. They're filled with stew made out of that deer I shot yesterday morning. Steam rises off the plates and the smell is good. She's a good cook, but that's not the only reason I stay.

She sets the plates down in front of each of them, puts a loaf of fresh-baked bread on each table, and then heads back for mine. I smelled that bread baking earlier while I was fixing the corral. She bakes bread every day, but it just smelled especially good this morning.

A stranger walks in the front door. He's sure been quiet. Normally, I can tell when someone sets foot on the porch, but this stranger just sort of appears. A big man. Maybe a full hand higher than me, and I'm six feet. Wide shoulders that slim down to his waist, where a Colt .45 hangs low on his right leg. The thong is off the hammer, but that doesn't mean anything, 'cause it's something any careful man would do, coming into a new place.

His clothes are dusty, especially his boots, so I figure he's been doin' some walking to get here. I notice there's a bunch of empty loops on his gun belt.

The Mexican sees him right away, and his fork stops for a second on its way up to his mouth. He sets the fork down beside his plate while he chews. It doesn't look like he did anything on purpose, but it does leave his gun hand free. I think I could like the Mexican without too much trouble.

The dude appears not to know the stranger is there, but I can tell he just doesn't really care. It must be nice not to have any enemies. The kid knows he's there, but keeps on eating, counting on the Mexican to keep an eye out, I guess.

Sarah carries my plate and loaf of bread out of the kitchen. She stops when she sees the stranger, then comes on over and sets it down in front of me. I notice she's careful not to get between the two of us. Smart woman.

His eyes follow her over, and flick to me for a long instant while he sizes me up. Then his eyes go back to her. Not that I blame him none. She's a sight better to look at than me, and that's for sure.

"Howdy, ma'am," he says.

"Hello," she comes back.

"Stew sure does smell fine." His voice is soft, but it carries real clear.

"Twenty-five cents to eat," she says.

He hesitates. "Twenty-five cents for stew?" he finally asks. I know he's broke. Been there myself a couple of times. "All right if I work it off?"

Sarah studies him for a minute. I know what she's going to do. She's going to feed him. She'd feed anybody that came through those doors, I think.

"Certainly," she says finally. "You sit and I'll fetch you a plate."

"Thank you, ma'am," he says. There's an empty table over in the corner by the door, and that's where he goes and sits down. Sarah's back in a minute with another plate of stew and half a loaf of bread. She sets them down in front of him and goes back for his cup. I know that must be half of her loaf, but Sarah's like that, you know.

He digs in, using his fork in a businesslike manner that tells me he hasn't eaten in a while.

We all hear the horses come up. Lots of horses . . . maybe six or seven. Eating stops pretty much while us men wait to see what's coming. Boots on the porch and men start coming through the door. Five, six, seven of them, and they are hunting. You can tell from the quick way they look around and study each of us. The thongs are off their guns and they're ready for business.

Sarah comes through the door, wonderment on her face, and I want to tell her to get out. But it's too late.

The stranger in the corner comes out of his chair like lightning, and his six-gun booms loud in the closed room. Two of the men yell in hurt surprise, and the rest grab their guns and start banging away. Some of them are shooting at the stranger and some at the other men who haven't done anything, as far as I can tell. The dude goes down without firing a shot, surprise on his face as he topples over backward. Guess sometimes being invisible just isn't good enough. One of them turns toward me and starts to raise his gun.

It's as far as he ever gets, 'cause my mama didn't raise no idiot children, and I yank my own pistol and go from eating to shooting right in the middle of a mouthful.

Two heavy .45 slugs bend him over in the middle, and he sits down on the floor real hard and just sort of bends forward as far as he can, and even though he's sitting upright,

I know he's dead. The sound of guns is real loud in the room, and powder smoke makes everything hazy and bites at my lungs, but not so hazy I can't see the kid on his knees, holding his belly and still trying to fire his piece. A shot to the face from one of them puts him the rest of the way out of the fight.

One of them saw me put his friend down and he fixes to turn his attention on me, and I have to take him out of it same as before. My gun bucks twice, and both shots slam home into his chest. I see his mouth twist in a curse, but his hands are already dead and they drop limply to his sides. He wobbles some for a second, and somebody else puts a bullet into him and he flips onto his back real hard.

There's only one man and me left standing, and he looks at me and I look at him, and I'm just a little bit faster. My lead smashes into his jaw and I hear him gurgle. My second shot smacks into his chest, and he half turns and falls to his face on the rough wood floor. He doesn't make any move to stop himself, and I can easy hear the smack as his face hits the floor, but I know it doesn't hurt him, 'cause he's dead.

The Mexican is spread out on the table. He makes some choking sounds and then relaxes.

The room is deadly silent except for the tinkle of brass hitting the floor and the click of my cylinder as I reload as quickly as I can.

And that's the way it happens. Everything peaceable and normal one minute, and then someone is dead and the room is full of smoke and the blood smell of copper.

I don't mind telling you that my heart is beating like a trip-hammer, bangin' away in my chest like it's trying to get out. As I look around, it occurs to me that my heart is the only one in the room still working at all, so I better not complain about its making a little noise.

My pistol is loaded again, all six cylinders, and I look the people all over, only it appears I won't need my gun any more this day. They are all dead with a capital *D,* and their troubles, whatever they were, are now behind them. Looking at all this death and dying makes me suddenly feel tired all over. Seems like I've already seen too many dead men.

I saw Sarah dash back into the kitchen when the fracas started, so I stuff my pistol back in the holster and walk slow and careful over to the door. I know she has a Greener double-barrel in there.

"Sarah," I say softly. "It's me."

"Is it over?" she asks.

I look over my shoulder at the dead men. "It surely is," I answer.

"Come on in, then," she says.

I walk around the corner and into her kitchen. She's sitting at the other side of her table with the Greener lying across the table. It feels kind of funny to be in her kitchen. I mean, I've never been in here before. It was always like her safe place for her and her alone. She nods at the chair across from her.

"Sit," she says. She talks real good, you know. She doesn't say "set" like most folks. She says "sit," pronouncing the *i* just as plain as can be. Educated woman. Her eyes are the clearest light blue, just like you can see right into her head. She has a little dusting of flour on her right cheek, and I want real bad to reach over and brush it off. But I don't.

She nods at the stove. "Coffee's hot," she says.

It doesn't even seem strange to me. I mean, here she is, sitting in a house with eleven dead men messing up the dining room, and she tells me the coffee is ready, and it seems like the natural thing for her to say.

I get a cup, pour it full, and then sit across from her, pretty close, and we're looking right into each other's eyes. Hers are light blue. Like crystals. Or maybe rock candy. Man could get lost in there and be proud to do it.

I sip easy at the hot cup and lean back, letting go a big sigh. The worry is running out of me, and I feel my tense muscles relax once more. I don't know for sure why I'm alive and everyone else is dead.

"What's your first name, Mr. Walker?" she asks me all of a sudden.

"John, ma'am."

"Middle name?"

"Thomas," I say. Funny, I've been here for three months and this is the first time she's ever asked me that.

"John T. Walker," she says kind of slow, making it sound real important somehow. I nod. "I like it," she says softly. "I like the way it rolls off the tongue."

I don't know what to say, so I don't say anything. Another sip hides my uneasiness.

"You have any family, John T. Walker?" she asks.

"No, ma'am," I respond. "Not anymore."

"I do," she says. "I have a daughter."

I am surely surprised. I mean, here she is, just a slip of a woman herself and she has a daughter already. Maybe they marry young back where she comes from. They marry at twelve and thirteen back in the hills of Tennessee, so I'm not surprised at that, I guess. Just that she never mentioned it before.

"I never had a husband," she says, just like she's making normal conversation. Now I am shocked. This is not the kind of thing that's talked about, especially out West. She must be awful upset to even say it, and I think maybe I'll just mosey on out of here before she says something that's so awful she won't be able to stand having me around anymore.

I set the cup back on the table and slide the chair back. She holds up a hand.

"Wait, John T.," she says. "Don't go."

She has a funny look in her eyes, but she sounds sincere, so I pick up the cup and sip again.

"It's not what you think, John T.," she says.

"What I think is that this is entirely your own business, ma'am," I say, "and I don't know if you should be telling me."

"Oh, yes," she says with a big sigh. "Now is the time for me to tell you this, all right."

"If you say so, ma'am." Seems like a strange conversation, what with eleven dead men cluttering up the next room, but she goes right on.

"She isn't a love child," Sarah says. It doesn't seem to bother her at all to be telling me this, but it sure is bothering *me*. "Her father is my stepbrother, Cyrus Weatherstone of Boston, Massachusetts. I guess living in the same house with me just got to be too much for him, and he was much bigger than I was."

I feel the fury rise in me as I imagine the big man forcing himself on a helpless girl.

She must be able to see it in my eyes, 'cause she smiles real gentle. "Thank you, John T.," she says, "but it's too late for that now. Besides, the ultimate result was Emily." She says the name real soft, almost like breathing instead of talking. "You should see her, John T., with beautiful yellow hair and blue eyes just like mine." She's quiet for a moment, and I can tell she's not in the kitchen anymore but back in Boston with her daughter. I sip at my coffee like I have all the time in the world, waiting for her to finish mind-traveling.

Sarah snaps back to the here and now all of a sudden. She even jerks as she becomes aware of me sitting there. "Sorry, John T.," she says.

I nod. I've never seen her so distant-like. Like she knows something I don't. Like normal things that hold a person back from telling things to others don't matter anymore.

"I have some money saved up," she says. "I planned to bring Emily out here."

"Pretty tough country for a young girl," I say, thinking about all those dead men in the next room.

"She'd have loved it out here," Sarah says. "You don't know what it's like back there, John. Noisy and busy and never peaceful." She looks toward the door. "I never knew what real silence was until I got out here," she goes on. "Real peace."

"Yes'm," I say. I don't know if this conversation is headed anywhere, but just as long as she can stand me this close, I'll sit here and listen.

"It was tough at first. Hard work and long days."

"This country is not too good on women alone," I agree.

"I made out finally. Somehow I managed, and the years just seemed to get away from me. I'm thirty-two, John. Did you know that?"

"No ma'am, I surely didn't." I am really amazed, but I don't let on. I never had any idea she was so much older than me. I mean, she's so pretty and alive and young-looking. Not that a few years would make any difference to me.

"Emily is fifteen now," she goes on. She gives a big sigh. "I wish I could see her once more." The longing in her voice is as plain as day.

"You'll see her again," I promise. She smiles at me real gentle, and my insides just plain melt. It's a wonderment that I just don't fall into a puddle on the floor.

"I'll never see her again," she whispers.

"Sure you will, ma'am."

She shakes her pretty head, clear blue eyes real serious.

"I caught one, John," she says.

"Ma'am?" I don't understand.

"A bullet came through that door and hit me in the stomach," she says in a calm, everyday voice.

My heart stops. I know I stop breathing. "What was that, ma'am?" I ask, not wanting to hear the answer.

She nods. "They got me, John. In the stomach."

I want to jump over the table and try to help, only her calm ways put me off. "Can I help?" My voice doesn't sound quite right.

"I don't think so. I saw a man who was shot in the stomach once. Nobody could help him. I don't think anybody can help me."

"You'd best let me have a look at it, ma'am," I say. *Please, God, don't let it be true!*

"If you wish, John."

I take her by the arm and we walk across the kitchen into her bedroom. I've never been in here before, and that's a fact.

Her bed is under the window, with no headboard or nothing. A gay blue and white quilt is arranged neatly over it. I help her to lie down on the quilt. There's a small hole in the front of her dress. She's gut-shot for sure. I've never felt sicker in my entire life.

"It doesn't hurt much," she says, "although I expect it will later."

It will. I've seen men die from wounds like that, and it wasn't pretty. It's bad enough to get shot and die. Worse to have to scream your life away, twisting and turning to get away from a pain you can't get away from.

It's like I'm all empty inside, and suddenly I realize that I've been having intentions toward this woman. Good intentions, mind you. Permanent intentions. If she would've had me. Only it's all gone now. The whole rest of my life is going to be spent without having her around. She'll be a memory I can bring out and think on when I'm alone, but she won't be real. She won't be a warm, living woman who might care about me. She'll just be someone alive in my mind.

I pull my knife out of my boot. "I better take a look at that wound, ma'am," I say.

"You're going to cut my dress?" She sounds distressed at the thought.

"Gonna have to. It's got a hole in it, anyway."

"Okay," she says, like it doesn't really matter anymore, and I guess it doesn't.

I keep my knife real sharp, and the calico splits in front of the blade almost like it's afraid of it. I pull the split cloth open. There it is, the bullet hole in her skin, and I can tell it angled deep into her innards, which means she's gonna die no matter what.

"How's it look?" she asks.

"Ain't so bad," I say.

From her smile, I can tell she knows the truth. I lay my hand on her belly. When a person's gut-shot, the first thing that happens is that the belly gets real hot. Then it swells up later. That's when the real pain comes. She's not too hot yet.

I'm surprised at how soft her skin is. I mean, her belly doesn't feel at all like mine. Its like there's a layer of softness underneath the skin just to make it warm and comfortable for a man to rest against. I am shocked and dismayed that I can even think about something like that while she's lying there on her deathbed.

"Your hand feels nice and warm," she says. "You've got a gentle touch."

I take my hand away from her. I know I have feelings for this woman, but it's too late.

"I used to lie here and think about you holding me," she says softly.

"You did?"

"Yes, John T., I did. Women are human too, you know."

I don't say anything. This day is becoming too much for one man to stand.

"I knew you'd be gentle," she goes on. "You're a good man, John."

"There's quite a few would argue with you, ma'am," I respond. "A couple of them are in the next room."

"Why'd you stay, John?"

"Ma'am?"

"Why didn't you move on like you always did before?"

"How did you know about me before?" I want to know.

"I just know what kind of man you are. How come you stayed here?"

I look down at her lying there on her pretty quilt, and I wish it was me down there and her up here. Only it's not. I know why I stayed.

And I want to tell her too. Only it's hard, a lot harder than I ever thought it'd be.

She waits patiently, like she has all the time in the world.

"Well, ma'am" is all I finally manage to get out.

"Tell me, John," she says. "I need to know."

I can feel my tongue getting thick and my mouth drying out. "Well, ma'am, I stayed . . . because . . . of you."

"I thought so. Do you love me, John?"

"I believe I do, Ma'am." It was a lot easier when she said it, and I just agreed.

She looks kind of satisfied when she hears that, like she was wanting it to be so only she wasn't quite sure. She moves a little bit and winces as a stab of hurt cuts through her. It tears me up inside to see her hurting and not be able to help her.

"I can't stand a lot of pain, John," she says.

"Ma'am, I have found that people can stand a lot more than they think."

"I have two favors to ask of you, John T.," she says.

A sickness washes over me, and I am sure the most miserable man on the face of the earth. "What's the second favor, ma'am?" I already know what the first is.

"I want you to fetch Emily out here," she says real calm, like she isn't asking anything at all.

"Fetch Emily from Boston, Massachusetts?"

I can hear the surprise in my own voice. The corners of her eyes crinkle slightly in a smile. Somehow, the clear blue seems to be cloudying up, almost like a mist is settling inside her.

"There's some money I've saved," she goes on. "It's in a jar under a rock halfway to the well on the left side of the path. See to it that she gets it, John."

I hear my voice say, "Yes, ma'am," and I'm surprised at myself. Maybe she doesn't know what she is asking, but *I* surely do.

"You give your word, John T.?" she asks.

"I give my word, Sarah," I say. It's the first time I ever called her that, and it sounds strange coming from my mouth.

"We have a little while yet," she says. "I want you to lie down here beside me and hold me."

So that's what I do. It seems as strange as can be, what with eleven men dead and stiffening in the next room, and her dying right there, and yet it feels real good too.

I slide my arm under her head and she sort of nestles up against me. She is warm and so soft, and she tries to sigh, but it catches in her throat as a stab of pain goes through her. She stiffens till it's over, then her breathing returns to normal.

"This is nice, John T.," she says softly.

We lie there like that, side by side, the living and the dying, until the sun is full down and the moon is risen. She gets worse as time goes on, and sometime after midnight she begins to cry.

I put my other arm around her and hold her as close as I can without hurting her even more, like I'm trying to hug the hurt and awful dread right out of her. Her arms go around me and she holds me close to her, only it really doesn't help much at all, and I can feel the hot drops of her tears fall on the side of my face.

I have never felt more helpless and hurt and angry, and all at the same time. Here, so close to me, is this woman I dearly love, and she's suffering worse than anyone can imagine, and I can do nothing to ease her agony. Her hot tears sear against my face, and I'm full up with feelings and have to get out of there before I explode.

I ease out from her hold.

"I'll be right back, Sarah," I promise. For a

second her hold is tighter, and I'm afraid she won't let me go. Then she releases her hold on me. I get up and walk to the door.

"Good-bye, John," she says. "I love you."

My eyes cloud up and brim over. "Good-bye, Sarah," I say even though it's my intention to return in just a minute or so. "I love you too."

I walk through the door and through the dining room, stepping around the stiffening bodies, and out the front door. The night air is cool and clean, and I breathe deep of it as I wait for my feelings to return to normal. Something doesn't feel regular, and my hand flashes down to my holster. It's empty.

The bang of my .45 cuts off a wolf in mid-howl, and I feel like I'm just as dead as my Sarah.

Chapter Two

I have never rode on a train before although I've seen them hurrying across the land and dragging their great plume of smoke along with them. I've felt the rails too, and you can tell when they're coming 'cause the rails buzz under your fingertips. But I never figured I'd ever have need to ride one of them.

The cars sort of jerk and sway as we race across the land faster than a horse can run sometimes, and they have soft seats and ride on springs. There are gaslights for when it gets dark, glass in the windows, and all in all it's maybe the finest place I've ever been.

There are many people on here with me. More than half the seats are full, and it's a surprise to me that with all these folks, I don't recognize anybody at all. They all have that surface friendliness of people who are stuck together someplace where they'd rather not be, but on the whole, they're not really friendly. I mean, what's the point? We're going to be companions for the length of the trip, but will prob'ly never run across each other ever again. I find something kind of sad about that attitude.

Some of these folk are prob'ly pretty nice people, honest and honorable. If a man were more outgoing, he might introduce himself to some of them and make lasting friendships. Only, you can tell from their faces that they're not interested, and so we all travel together but are all alone. I think maybe this will be a long journey. 'Course, I'll have company coming back. I'm looking forward to meeting Miss Emily.

About that night. I took care of all the horses. Then I lay there with Sarah until morning, when the sound of Jess Wright blowing his horn rousted me away from her and out to greet him. It maybe doesn't sound right, my lying there with a dead woman, but it felt right and that's that.

So I heard his horn and I got up. It was almost a surprise to walk through the front room and see all those dead men. The business with Sarah had clean put them from my mind. I'd have to say that maybe Jess and his passengers were a lot more surprised than I was, though.

Jess is a pretty smart fellow, and he walked through the station and it didn't take much time for him to put together what had happened. He never did talk to me much, but when we got to Sarah lying in her bed and the messed-up spot next to her where I had been, he looked at her for a minute and then at me before he turned and walked out.

The passengers were a different story, though. At first they were nervous, like most folks are around dead people. Then Jess told them pretty much what had happened, and they came down on me like I was something holy and they wanted to get as close as they could. I tell you, it made me darned nervous to have them carrying on about me. They all seemed proud about how I was so good with a gun. I don't know what they were so excited about, because I killed only three of those dead men myself.

We buried them right there behind the station and put wood crosses over them. I didn't know any names to put on them, so Sarah's is the only one with a name. Jess carved it in there real good, and put a big R.I.P. down the long way. It looks real nice, what with the *R* in Sarah also being the *R* in R.I.P.

And so we shoveled dirt on them—the hungry stranger, the crusty Mexican, the shiny dude, the kid, the men who killed them and the men they killed. Sarah too. Side by each they are buried, and there must be some lesson there, only I don't know what it could be. It's better to be alive than dead—that's what it boils down to.

Nobody seems real sure what all the shooting was about, and the only people who could say are not talking anymore. I think it was about money, on account of the map I found on the hungry stranger. Accident that I found it, really. If he'd been shot someplace else, I never would have seen it under his shirt.

It wasn't much, just a piece of deerskin with some writing on it. There was one picture of a pool or a lake and a couple of other circles that must be hills. Lots of writing, though. And it has a star on it. A dotted line from one of the circles leads right to the star, and I guess that star is the whole reason for the map to be in the first place. But I don't know what is at the star. And it has lots of writing on it.

There's something magical about a map when a man doesn't know where it leads or what is waiting at the other end. It tugs at his mind, and a man can imagine 'most anything, from gold mines to buried bank loot. Or it could be nothing at all, just a good place to camp or a place with fresh water, which would be a lot more likely than something of value. Nobody knows I have it, and it's my intention to track it down the first chance I get.

As for Sarah's money, I found it just like she said—a hundred and thirty-four dollars. It doesn't seem like much for a whole life, but I bet it seemed a fortune to her. Anyhow, it weighs like a lot more than a hundred and thirty-four dollars in my inside vest pocket, and I'll be glad to get rid of it.

I haven't figured out exactly how I'm going to get Emily to come out with me. I'm not even certain that I should. I mean, what's an Eastern girl going to do out West without a man? It doesn't bear thinking on. I might not be doing her any favor, but that's what Sarah wanted, and that's what I gave my word to, so I'll do it somehow.

'Course, any child would want to do her ma's last wish, so I expect she'll come. It's not going to look too good, her traveling with a man she's not married to, but I'll take care of her the best I can, and I wouldn't take kindly to any nasty remarks from disapproving folks.

"Excuse me. Is this seat taken?"

It's a skinny man standing in the aisle. I know it's not nice to say things about people that don't put the best shine on them, but this man is really and truly scrawny. No other word for it. Tall, with big hands that don't seem to fit on his frame.

"Nope," I answer. "It surely is not." I take my feet down from the seat.

"Thank you, sir," he says, and sits down across from me. He pretends to be looking out the window, but I can tell he's looking me over real good in the glass.

There's not too much for him to see here, only six feet of man, pretty wide across the shoulders, and a face that's put fear into lots more people than it has charmed. My skin's tanned and tough from the weather I been out in my whole life. Not dressed too good, I prob'ly just look like any other cowboy. I guess he's satisfied, on account of he reaches out his hand.

"Name's Justice," he says. "Rufus Justice."

I take his hand and shake it. His grip is not too good, so I hold back a mite. "Howdy," I answer.

He takes his hand back, and I notice he wipes it on his pants right away. Actually, it's not really necessary, on account of my hands are clean. I washed them in the fancy gentlemen's room at the end of the car when I was exploring the train.

"I'm from Boston," he announces.

"That's where I'm going," I respond.

"Really?" He manages to sound interested. "Business or pleasure trip?"

Now, that's not really the kind of question you ask out West. Only, I can see he's trying to be polite, not nosy.

"Business," I say right back. "But, since I've never been there before, I guess I'll look around some."

"A good idea," he responds. "Plenty to see in Boston." Only, he doesn't say it like *Boston*. More like *Baastan*.

"I've heard that," I say. "I heard they even have a place where there are all kind of books and you can just walk on in and look at any you please."

"Ah, yes, the library," he comes back. "Are you a reader, sir?"

Now, that for sure is not a good question to ask out here, but he appears so interested and friendly that I don't take offense.

"I would like to be," I answer. "I have never had the chance before, but if there really is such a place, I believe I'll give it a try. Lots of folk read, so it can't be all that hard. I should be able to pick it up in an afternoon." He smiles at that, I don't know why.

I am thinking of the map I found. Lots of writing and not enough pictures for me to tell where anything really is, and I'm leery of asking anybody to help.

"You work in Boston, do you?" I ask.

"Indeed I do, sir. I am a physician."

"Well, now, that's interesting. I've done a little cutting and sewing myself."

"I expect that's quite common out here," he comes back. "Wild country, where a man must make do to survive." He sighs and leans back. "Sometimes, sir, I envy you men of the West. You can concern yourself with the basics of survival and ignore the fanciful behaviors of so-called civilization."

I like him, scrawny or no. He's an educated man, yet he doesn't talk down to me like so many others have. I know I'm not so smooth with words, but he looks past them and studies on what I'm trying to say. This trip may not be so bad after all. Maybe I can study on his manners and pick up a little of that civilization he's not so crazy about.

"For example, take that business at the Mindowan stage station," he goes on. "*There* was a man in a predicament. Eleven men trying to kill him, and only his skill and speed stood between him and death. Amazing as it seems, he managed to bring all eleven down without getting so much as a scratch. Walker, that's his name. I'm sure you heard of it. Everybody has. That's the kind of action and freedom I'm talking about." He sighs. "I should dearly enjoy meeting that man."

"I heard it a little different," I say.

His eyebrows go up in interest, but he keeps right on talking about how I was supposed to have killed all eleven of those men. Seems like he's trying to make me out to be one of those steely-eyed killers from the dime novels. I wait until he has to stop for a breath, and then I butt right in.

"There was a woman killed there too," I point out.

"Ah, yes. Most unfortunate."

"She had blue eyes," I say.

He looks startled. "You knew her?" he asks.

"Yes."

"I'm sorry." And he really sounds sorry.

"Me too, Doc," I say.

"I didn't get your name."

"John," I shoot right back. "My name's John T."

"Nice to meet you, Mr. Tee," he comes back with, and it doesn't seem important enough to correct him. Besides, it might make him squirmy to find out he's riding with the hard-eyed killer of eleven men.

We stop for food just before dark. We go into a large building where there are long tables already set with plates and eating utensils. Surly waiters bring out the beans and potatoes and beef that's almost tough enough to get up and walk back to their old ranch. They tromp around again with some fruit pie, but I'm hard put to name the kind of fruit, and the coffee is worse than range coffee 'cause it's all watery and full of old grounds.

They give us thirty minutes to enjoy this fine repast. Then the whistle blows and we all head back to the train. People ate a lot better back at the old stage station, and I think about Sarah and am somber and quiet as I sit down in the train.

We start out with a hard jerk that has all the passengers bowing to one another, and the land begins to move past the window once more.

The food has sort of slowed down everybody, and they gradually begin to nod off, heads bobbing right along with the train. Just after the conductor comes around and lights the lamps, a young man comes around and tries to sell us stuff. He has apples and a newspaper that he says is printed right on the train. He has books and even claims to have one from France with racy pictures of women for which he is asking two whole dollars. Doc and I don't buy anything, and he finally moves on. Persistent young fellow, though.

It gradually gets darker and darker outside, and the warm glow of the lights turns the windows into black mirrors so the only thing you can see in them is yourself looking back. No moon out there, and we might as well be traveling through a barrel of tar for all you can see.

The hours jerk by, and I, too, pull my hat down over my eyes and try to sleep. Someday, somebody is going to figure out how to make a train car full of beds where a body can lie down and get a proper rest, I expect, but for now, we can only try to stretch out and sleep as best we can. I'm beginning to get an inkling about just how long this trip is going to be.

The trip is supposed to take three days, but it takes four, what with all the unscheduled stops for other trains in the way, and busted rails, and the like. At times we're doing all of thirty miles in an hour, and it's truly amazing that the big shiny engine doesn't ever get tired. I think maybe that when they get this railroad business all figured out and working right, there might be a whole bunch of horses and coaches going begging.

Every time we stop at a station, some folks get off and others get on. The farther East we get, the more duded up the other passengers are, until just looking at them makes me feel kind of plain. Maybe a little worse than plain. But my clothes are paid for, and the mends are caused by wear and tear from hard work, so I guess maybe I'm not shamed by the way I look after all.

I could have taken some of my money and got new clothes, but I learned a long time ago that you might as well be who you are, because one way or another you're going to show through, anyhow. Like Doc here. He'd like to be hard and cold like he thinks Westerners are, but he's been so many years taking care of folks that he doesn't hardly have any hard and cold left in him. I like him for that.

We keep company for the trip, mostly him talking and me listening, sort of closing out the rest of the folks on the train. He talks a lot about medicine and people he has helped, and once in a while about the unfortunate ones he was not able to save. Some of them happened years ago, but I can tell they still prey on his mind. There's a big load on a man when he takes it into his head to become a doctor, I think.

At the end of our trip I have to put him in that very small group that I consider friends. I can tell he favors me too, maybe partly because he sees me as a romantic cowboy, but also on account of he really likes me.

I let him in on that I'm going to Boston to meet a girl and give her the legacy left by her mother. He doesn't ask any questions, just accepts that, and that's another of the reasons I like him.

The Boston station is grand. That is the only way I know how to describe it. It's even bigger than Clintwood's Hotel back in Virgil, and alive with people all hurrying to get to and from somewhere. Doc and I stand on the platform for a minute and watch the tearful hello of a mother who's been waiting for her son to get off the train. She puts her arms around him even though he's full grown, and she's crying without making any noise about it. The sight makes me have that feeling deep down I get once in a while whenever I think about being all alone in the world. No matter how tough a man can look on the outside, being alone makes for a bitter feeling in the gut sometimes. I try not to think on it much, and turn to Doc.

"Nobody coming to meet you?" I ask.

"No," he says. "My wife passed on three years ago, and there are no children."

It's the first time he has mentioned anything about his family and I want him to know I'm sorry. "Bet she was a good woman," I say.

He smiles a little, and his face gets kind of a warm look on it as he thinks back on her. "That she was, John," he says with feeling. He looks at me. "You got any place to stay, John?"

It still feels funny to have someone calling me John. Seems like folks have been calling me Walker my whole life.

"Nope," I admit. "I figure there must be a rooming house or maybe a hotel in a town this size." I don't know why that makes him smile, but it does.

"Why don't you come and stay with me," he suggests. "I have plenty of room, and you could search out your young lady just as easily from my house as from anyplace else."

I ponder on that, and although I'd hate to put anyone out, it doesn't seem like a bad idea.

"That's real nice, Doc," I respond. "Hospitality like that is what you'd expect of a Westerner." He kind of lights up at that, but it's true. Out West, you have to help each other out. I never sent a man away from my fire hungry, even if it meant we both had to shorten rations some. I've never been sent away from any camp hungry, either, even though sometimes I didn't like the people much and they didn't like me much, either.

I still feel kind of undressed, what with my gun tucked away in my carpetbag, but Doc has told me I shouldn't wear it around Boston, 'least not where everybody can see it right out. He says only the law walks around armed, and I guess maybe that isn't such a bad idea, only it sure wouldn't work out West. A man's gun is like a tool out there. Just something he has belted on in case he needs to use it to kill a snake or something to eat. Or to kill a man who needs killing.

Seems like I've been wearing a gun ever since Mr. Devroe picked me out of the ashes of my parents' cabin and healed me and took me to be his own. I wasn't hardly out of bed more than a week when he gave me my first gun and started teaching me how to use it.

He was right fond of guns on account of he sold them. Pretty handy with one too, and he trained me to be the same, so I could be of help to him should he ever need it. I would have been too, only there were too many of them and they held me tight while they shot into him over and over again and he went down. It made me sick to see him fall, him being like a father to me, and I never will forget the sound the bullets made as they smacked into him.

After it was over they let me go, so I took and buried him just outside that godless town. I loaded myself down with some of his selling guns, and my own too. Then I walked back into that tavern where they were still drinking and I let her fly. There were eight of them and one of me, but I was in the right and powerful angry, and when it was over, the tavern was shot to pieces and so were they. I took two bullets, but they weren't so bad. That's why I limp now and again, depending on the weather.

Nobody knew my name, of course. I was just the kid with Devroe, and that's what they called me after the word got around—the kid at the Broken Branch. I've never told anybody about that before, but I guess it's old news and doesn't matter anymore.

After the shooting was over, I walked away and got on my horse and took Devroe's horse and stuff and left. Nobody followed me, and nobody ever knew I was the one. It seems like a good idea to keep that all quiet and forgotten, and so I have for these eight years. Funny how I got involved in another shooting mess just like that again. Maybe I'm a bad seed and trouble just looks for me.

Now, at the railroad station in Boston, Doc and I walk through all the people and go outside where there are a bunch of carriages waiting to take folks where they want to go.

"Corner of Baker and Broad," Doc says to the driver, and we get inside and the driver clucks at his horse and we're off into the city of Boston.

I've never seen so many houses and buildings all together like that in my whole life, and I gawk just like a kid. I catch Doc smiling at me once or twice, but I know he's not laughing at me, and I don't mind.

There are men and women everywhere, walking on boardwalks made out of cement. The streets are made of brick, and I can't begin to imagine where they ever got so many of them. The wheels rumble as they roll over them, and there are many streets that branch out from the one we are on, and they all have houses and stores and buildings along them. I think this city may be bigger than I first thought.

The women catch my eye, of course. There are so many of them, more than I have ever seen at one time before, and they're out walking with their menfolk or sometimes even alone. Mostly they have on big, pretty dresses and carry funny cloth umbrellas, and some of them are strikingly pretty. Doc hardly seems to pay them any mind at all.

It takes us about twenty minutes until we pull to a stop and get out. We're not in such a busy part of Boston anymore. Lots of big trees line the street on both sides, and we're in front of a grand house with fancy woodwork around the roof and a wrought-iron fence around the outside. There's a large porch on the front with a hanging swing, and a person is looking out the front window at us.

"I thought you didn't have anybody," I say to Doc as the carriage pulls away.

"I don't," he says. "I do have some servants who take care of the place for me."

"Servants?" I'm surprised. I've never even seen a servant before.

"Yes," he says, "a cook, a maid, and a man-servant to help out around the place."

"How they going to feel about you bringing a stranger home with you?"

He laughs. "Don't worry, my friend. They'll get used to you soon enough, and I feel you shall get used to them. You may even get to like it after a while."

I don't know how I'm going to like living with servants. Seems like a man ought to be free to take care of himself instead of waiting on someone else. We walk through the metal gate and on up to the porch. Doc had left his luggage on the ground where the driver set it. I got my carpetbag with me, though. The front door opens.

"Good evening, sir," says this big guy with a funny way of talking.

"Good evening, James," Doc says. I can see the big guy looking me over from the corner of his eye. He's wearing a black suit and looks like an undertaker. In the middle of the day, no less. "We'll be having a guest," Doc tells him. "This is Mr. John Tee, and he will be staying with us for a while."

James doesn't even bat an eye. "Very well, sir," he says in that same tone.

He steps aside and Doc motions me in. First thing that happens is this James fellow tries to take my carpetbag from me. We have a private tug-of-war right there in the doorway.

"Let me put that in your room, sir," he finally says.

I look at Doc, who's grinning fit to bust.

"I think you can let him have it," he says.

"Just a minute," I say to James, and I take my holster and gun out of the bag. "*Now* you can have it," I say. His eyes get bigger when he sees the gun and cartridge belt, but I don't know why, because it's just an ordinary Colt like so many others. He stiffens in disapproval.

"I can assure you, sir, that you will not need that weapon here," he says.

I do like to hear him talk. He speaks English good enough, only he makes his words sound so very, very important.

"I'll be the judge of that," I say, and I hear Doc snort behind me. I don't know what he thinks is so funny.

"As you wish, sir," James bites off, and it

looks like the first round goes to me. "If you'll follow me, I'll show you to your room," he says over his shoulder.

With a last glance at Doc, I follow him up the curving staircase. It's all polished wood, glowing dark and rich. I think maybe Doc is a little better off than he lets on, not that I'm complaining. It's a lot better to be rich and not show it than to be proud without any reason.

The guest room is outfitted better than the Clintwood Hotel back home. There's a big bed with a fancy headboard and a down quilt, and also two sitting chairs with fabric that matches the heavy drapes on the two windows. A dry sink sports a pretty pitcher and basin, and there's a clean white towel hanging there that nobody has ever used before. A brand-new bar of soap lies in a pretty little dish behind the basin.

I toss my gun belt on the bed. "Elegant," I say. "Elegant!" I heard Travis Able say that once when he was telling about a St. Louis Hotel.

"I'm pleased that it meets your approval, sir," the servant says back, almost like he really means it.

I figure that since we're going to be living

together, it might be a good idea to clear the air, if you know what I mean.

"Listen, Mr. . . . Mr. . . ."

"You may call me James, sir," he fills in the empty spot.

"Okay, James," I say. "You can call me John." It only seems fair.

"Certainly, Mr. Tee," he responds.

"We're going to be living together in this house for a while and so I think we should understand each other. I'm a Western man, and while I might want to be as right and mannerly as you, it has been my misfortune to be raised in a harsh land by harsh rules. Some of the things I do will doubtless seem hard and unmannerly to you, but I want you to know now that I don't mean them as such. I am asking you not to take offense at my actions, on account of I wouldn't likely know why you were doing so." It's a long speech for me, and I can't remember when I went to so much trouble to stay on a man's good side.

James seems slightly surprised. Well, I tried. If he didn't get my drift, I guess the two of us will just have to tolerate each other.

"I understand, Mr. Tee," he says, as prim

and proper as ever, which doesn't really tell me anything at all. "Dinner will be in one hour, sir." And then he leaves, closing the door behind him.

I'm glad to know when we get fed, but it doesn't ever take me anywhere near an hour to wash my hands, and I'm ready to go back downstairs real quick. Out of respect to Doc, I leave my Colt in the room. Anyhow, I got my bowie slid in my boot.

I get to the bottom of the curved stairs. There's a hall leading deeper into the house, and there are doors on both sides. All the doors are closed. Now what?

Just then, the door at the far end of the hall swings open and James comes out carrying a tray with a single glass of wine. He spies me right away and looks at me sort of like a man seeing a worm on his plate.

"The doctor is in the study," he says. "If you'll follow me. . . ." And he walks up to the first door at the end of the stairs on the south side of the hall. I would follow him, only the door he just came through doesn't slam shut but swings to and fro just like the door in a saloon. This wouldn't be a puzzlement, except that from where I am,

I can't see any hinges. I walk to the door and give it a little shove.

Sure enough, it swings back and forth a couple of times. I study it, because I have always liked to see how things work. It has been a weakness of mine since I took apart my first handgun as a youth.

The door swings on a pivot that comes up from the end of the door, but I can't see any reason why it should return to the closed position every time like it does. I shove it again, harder this time. A squeal and crash of glass from the other side leads me to believe I've just made my first social error in Doc's home.

Real gentle, I pull the door open toward me.

First thing I see is a brown pudding splayed out on the polished wood floor, all surrounded with busted glass dishes and such. Right behind the pudding is standing a pair of feet in plain brown shoes. I sort of follow up the gray dress and white apron. A pair of young woman's hands are fisted up and jammed on her hips, and when I get up to the face, her expression suggests that I might just be better off if I let the door swing closed again.

"Sorry, ma'am," I say. But I don't get any further.

"You're sorry!" she starts off. "Do you have any idea how long I worked on that mousse?" Before I can answer, she keeps right on going. I don't know anything about any moose. Her eyes flash up and down me, and it's plain she's not much impressed with what she's seeing. "We don't need any more outside help! And you should know enough to come to the back door!" She suddenly catches sight of James coming up behind me.

"James," she says, "please show this . . . this . . . gentleman out." First time I ever heard the word "gentleman" used as a cuss word.

James sort of clears his throat. "Harumph!" he says.

She is kind of a cute little thing, especially when she's angry and there's fire in her eyes. She is maybe about the same age as me, although it's hard to tell on account of her being so angry. When women are angry, they sort of look older than they really are. Her hair is done up in a bun thing tied tight at the back and it is plain brown. Her eyes are brown too, and they are right next to the cutest little button nose you ever did see. Her mouth is a thin, hard line right now, but that's on account of she's mad as a hornet, I think.

"Ma'am," I butt in afore James can have his say, "while nothin' would please James more, he can't show me out on account of I'm here with Doc himself. I'm invited to stay here until my business in Boston is completed."

I almost have to smile as I watch her expressions change one after the other. She goes through the whole range, just about. From anger to doubt to questioning to acceptance to blushing. Doesn't take her any time at all, either.

"You sure do look better when you're blushing than when you're angry," I point out. She does too.

'Course, that just makes it worse, and she gets redder and spins around and practically runs back into the kitchen.

James is looking at me kind of funny.

"I always had a way with women," I say to him. For an instant I could swear he almost smiled, but I must be wrong, 'cause his expression never really changes.

Chapter Three

James leads me into what he calls the study, where Doc is sitting behind a desk going through a bunch of letters that must have come while he was gone. There's quite a pile of them, and I cannot help but be impressed on account of I never got a single letter from anybody in my whole life. 'Course, I suppose a lot of them must be people paying their bills and such, but it must be a thrill to have somebody who cares enough to send a letter.

"Hello, John," he says, and even though I just left him a few minutes ago, he's glad to see me. He puts aside his mail and comes out from behind the desk where he motions me to an easy chair.

"Sit down and make yourself at home," he says. "James, I'll have a whiskey and water."

"Very good, sir," James drones right back, then turns to me. "And you, sir?" he asks.

I normally just drink beer when I drink anything at all, only it doesn't seem quite dignified enough for the occasion.

"I'll have the same, if you don't mind," I say.

"Certainly, sir," he responds. The words are polite enough, but his attitude is so distant it's like I don't exist at all. I don't think he likes me much. 'Course, maybe that's the way a good servant is supposed to act. He goes back out.

"What was all the noise?" Doc asks as he sits down in the chair next to me.

"I guess I owe you an apology. I pushed open a door in the hall and some woman dropped a pudding on the floor. The dishes she was carrying are what made all the noise. Far as I can tell, the pudding did not make any sound at all."

He laughs out loud. "Do not worry, my friend," he says. "Dishes can be replaced."

"That's what I thought," I say back. "If you let me know how much they cost, I'll be sure to send you the price."

"Won't hear of it," he says.

The door opens and James comes in carrying a tray with two drinks. Doc takes one and I take the other. James leaves the room. I take a sip.

"I don't think James has a high opinion of me," I say.

"James is an excellent butler," Doc says. "It's considered to be quite an honorable profession in England, where he is from. His father was a butler and so was his father's father, and so forth. One of the characteristics of good butlering is that they should remain unobtrusive, cool, and calm at all times. I think that what you are interpreting as dislike is merely his unemotional attitude."

"Could be," I say to be agreeable, but in spite of what Doc just said, James doesn't care for me much, I'm thinking.

We sip our drinks in a companionable silence, two friends pretty much at ease one with the other. It's not long before James is back.

"Dinner is served," he announces. About time too, since I'm definitely empty clean through. We finish up our drinks and follow James down the hall to the last door on the left. He holds the door for us to go through.

I have never seen anything like it and stop dead to take it all in. The room fairly glows with the sight of highly polished wood. It even comes halfway up the walls and practically reeks with clean. There are white curtains on the two windows, and they're matched by a large table in the center of the room that has a clean white cloth. The table is set with two places, one at each end, and between them are two candle holders with five lit candles in each.

James pulls back a chair for Doc and even spreads a cloth across Doc's lap, in case he should spill anything, I suppose. Then he walks to the other end and pulls back the chair for me.

Now, I have to admit I feel like a pig studying on a pan full of pork chops. I have never had another man hold a chair for me. As I go over and sit down, I'm suddenly aware of how shabby my clothes look in this fancy house.

A man's hand darts down toward my lap and I instinctively grab it by the wrist. I am suddenly eyeball to eyeball with James, our faces real close together. We look at each other for a long instant, and his eyes are absolutely expressionless, although I somehow feel that, inside, he's laughing his head off at me.

"Your napkin, sir," he says, and I sheepishly let go of his wrist and this grown man spreads a white cloth on my lap. Bet he thinks I'll fill it up with slobbered food too. But I'll fool him there, on account of I hardly ever drool. I'm afraid, though, I will doubtless find another way to make a fool of myself and then advertise the fact to everybody present.

The other door swings open and the girl who tried to throw me out comes in carrying a big covered bowl. She does not look at me as she goes over and stands beside Doc. I'm sure making some kind of an impression on Doc's servants.

James dips out some soup and puts it in Doc's bowl. Then they come around and serve me too. That done, they both go back into the kitchen. Doc takes a spoonful of his soup, and I try to eat mine the same as him. Seems like we're spooning backward, but if that is good enough for him, it's good enough for me.

"You always eat this formal?" I finally ask. I must admit the soup was delicious.

He smiles at me from around the candle holders. "No," he says. "I think they're trying to impress you because you're my guest."

"They surely have," I say back, and it's true. They have impressed me so much I'm likely to starve to death for fear of doing something wrong.

Doc tinkles a little bell, and in they come to take out our used dishes and bring in more food. It's roast beef and very good, only I just cannot seem to eat under these conditions. It is just so—so—sanitary and impersonal.

Dessert is sliced fresh peaches in heavy cream, and finally dinner is over and we can retire to the sitting room.

According to what Doc found out, Cyrus Weatherstone lives about a half mile away on Wedgwood Avenue. He says it's a small street that doesn't go anywhere at all. A "dead-end street" is what he calls it, and those might be true words if I run into that evil man there.

Not that I'm looking for trouble. I am not. One thing I've learned in my years on this earth is that killing someone else is not going to help bring back anybody who is already dead. On the other hand, it would give me great satisfaction to put a hole through the man who caused my poor dead Sarah so much pain and travail.

I say my good night early and make my way up to my room. The bed is turned down and there's fresh water in the pitcher, so I take the pleasure of washing my face and arms. Seems like a shame to dirty that small towel, but I wipe myself dry.

The floor squeaks just outside my room and I soft-foot over and take my pistol to hand. There's a quiet knock on the door, and after a moment of hesitation I pull it open. There on the floor is a tray with a thick slice of beef between two slices of bread. There's also a chunk of cheese and a bowl of peaches and cream. Looks like I won't have to go to sleep hungry after all.

I move the pitcher over and drag a chair up to the small table. The sandwich is delicious. I take another bite and think on who brought it. I know who it was, on account of I saw her head with its tightly pulled back hair going down the stairs as I opened the door.

When I get up at first light, there is not much goin' on. In fact, I can't hear anybody moving around at all, so I try to be real quiet. It is already a half hour past dawn, and I can't believe all these folks are sleeping in so late and it's not even Sunday.

I quiet-step down the stairs and across the hall. Through the swinging door, I head for the one that opens into the kitchen. When I listen for a second, I can hear someone moving around inside, so they are not all slugabeds. I push open the door and go in.

The kitchen is big, with a black cast-iron stove that is maybe one of the finest I've ever seen. There's a black woman standing there and spooning coffee into the pot.

" 'Morning," I say.

She lets out a yelp and spins around pretty good for a woman her size. "I know you," she says. "You're Mr. Tee, our guest. I'm Macy."

I raise an eyebrow at her. I for sure haven't seen her before.

"I peeked at you through the dining-room door last evening," she explains. "I had to see who it was got Miss Nancy so upset." She looks me over pretty good while I'm standing there. "Kinda threadbare," she pronounces, "but prob'ly honest and a hard worker."

"Thank you kindly," I say. "I've seen worse headstones than that."

She laughs, a nice big laugh from a nice, big, fat woman. "You have a seat there by the table," she says. "I'll get you a cup of coffee from my own pot. Maybe we'll talk a bit."

"Coffee sounds fine, but I'm not much of a talker. Good listener, though."

"Never enough of those around," she says as she sets a steaming cup of coffee in front of me. It smells real good, and my first sip tells me it tastes as good as it smells.

"You hungry already?" she asks.

"Yes'm," I say. "I'm normally fed and working by this time."

She plops some bacon into a fry pan and in no time at all the smell of bacon fills the kitchen.

"You need some wood brought in?" I offer.

"You just sit," she says. "Doc has people to do for me. It's for me to do for you, because you're a guest in his home," she explains.

I don't want to make any more social mistakes, so I do like she says and just sit.

"Miss Nancy, she said you was foolin' with the door," she says.

"Yeah," I admit. "I never saw one like that before, and I was trying to understand how it worked. Didn't mean any harm."

So the girl was named Nancy. Kind of a plain name, but, then, she didn't seem anything special, either. On the surface, at least.

"Miss Nancy works here, does she?"

Macy nods. "She's an orphan the doctor took in. Her folks were both killed in an accident at the factory where they worked. Doc tended to them that night, and all the others too, but he couldn't save them."

The back door opens and in comes the girl, all bright and fresh.

" 'Morning, Macy," she says. " 'Morning, Mr. Tee." We both say howdy right back. "Surprised to see you in here so early," she says to me.

"I was always an early riser."

"Is it true that you are a man of the West?" she asks as she gets herself some coffee.

"Born and raised," I reply.

"And do you carry a gun all the time and kill men?"

She has been reading dime novels, I bet. "I carry a gun, ma'am. All of us do. But it's a tool. No more'n no less."

"And please tell me why you found it necessary to pull this weapon on James yesterday."

I must admit I'm a little surprised. I seem to have been the object of some discussion when I wasn't around.

"Ma'am, I didn't pull my gun on James. I just value it some, so I took it from my bag before I let a stranger walk away with it."

"Well, you're in Boston now, Mr. Tee," she goes on like she's talking to a child. "You can get in trouble waving a weapon around in this city."

I think maybe she's a little snippy, and I don't like her a whole lot. "Thank you kindly for the warning, ma'am," I respond. Even as I speak, I can feel the pressure of where I have tucked the gun in the back of my trousers where my coat will cover it. I finish my coffee and set the cup on the table. Macy sets a plate of eggs and bacon in front of me and I realize I am hungry to the core. I commence to eating and am soon finished.

"I must be going," I say. "Thank you for the breakfast, Macy."

"You're welcome, Mr. Tee. Come back here anytime you've a mind to."

"I think I should come with you," Nancy says. "You don't know the city and you might get lost." I don't like the idea of taking this slip of a girl with me on my job, but she's right. I don't know the city or the ways of the city, and I could use the services of someone who does.

"If it wouldn't be too much bother, I could use the company," I say, and away we go.

Doesn't seem like any time at all and we're walking in the road together. She's a fast walker and it's not but fifteen minutes when she says, "This is Wedgwood Avenue, Mr. Tee." They are the first words she has spoken since we left the house, but it wasn't a harsh quiet between us. More like we just didn't have anything to say to each other and no need to say it.

"Which one belongs to Cyrus Weatherstone?" I ask.

She looks at me in surprise. "It's right there," she says. "Right where it says Judge C. Weatherstone."

"Oh," I say, and study the three houses that face out on the little stub of a street. All of them have signs in front with writing on them, and none of them have a picture on the sign to give a man a clue as to what the writing says.

"Come along," she says real quick, like she doesn't know I can't read, only I can tell she just figured it out. It bothers me some. This snip of a girl can do something I cannot, and it's galling. I follow her down to the third house and through the gate. She uses the knocker on the door with vigor, and we wait for a minute. The door opens and it is Sarah's daughter who opens it.

There is no doubt it's Sarah's daughter, on account of her eyes are almost the same shade as her mother's were, and her nose and mouth are almost the same too.

"Hello, Emily," I say.

She's puzzled, and looks from us one to the other. "Hello," she says. "Do I know you?"

"No, you don't, but I feel like *I* know *you*. I knew your mother and promised her I would come here." It's a long speech for me.

"You know my mother?"

"Yes. I knew her pretty good, I guess."

She opens the door wide. "Please come in, Mr. . . . ?"

"Tee," Nancy says. "John Tee."

The parlor is full of furniture and pictures and such. There's a piano next to the wall, and the curtains are made of velvet. We all sit down. I'm not real comfortable. I haven't been in a room like this since me and George Wall was in the dance hall down by Walker's Creek. I didn't do anything wrong there, mind you. I was never inside one of them before and we sort of dared each other to go in. 'Course, I was a lot younger then.

"Please tell me about my mother," Emily says.

I've been waiting and getting ready for that question for a long time. "Your mother was a fine lady—" is as far as I get.

"What do you mean 'was'?" Emily wants to know, which gives me a bad feeling.

"You mean you don't know?" I ask. She shakes her head.

There is no good way to tell her this. "Your mother is dead," I say as gently as I can. I can see the shock in her clear blue eyes. Seems like only a short time ago I was watching the life go out of eyes just like that.

Emily puts her hand to her heart. "Dead?" she says. "Mother is dead?"

"Yes," I say. "She's dead and buried proper, with a marker over her head that says R.I.P." We all sit there for a while. I'm in no hurry to go on. Takes some time for a person to get used to news like that.

"Please go on," she finally says. "I want to hear about her. I really don't remember much about her."

"Your mother was a fine woman," I start again, but then a man comes into the room. He is a big man with a potbelly, boasting a fat gold watch chain draped across it from one vest pocket to the other.

"Good morning, Emily," he says. "Who are your friends so early in the morning?"

"Good morning, Uncle Cyrus," she says, and I take a sudden interest in the man. It is him, the despoiler of my Sarah, an evil man who will bear watching.

"This is Mr. and Mrs. John Tee," she introduces us to him. A shocked expression crosses Nancy's face at being identified as my wife, but she doesn't say anything. "They have come to tell me about Mother. She's dead, Uncle."

His gaze sharpens and he looks at us hard. "You knew Sarah?" he asks. I nod. "And she told you about Emily?"

"She told me *all* about her," I say harshly, and now he knows that I know about his dirty secret. There's a silence that seems explosive and overlong, and his face hardens while his eyes narrow. I have seen that look before, and if he had a gun, he'd be fixin' to use it.

"I want you out of my house," he says, and his tone lets on that he means it.

"I believe you," I say right back, and I get up and motion Nancy to her feet.

"Uncle!" Emily says. "I don't understand."

"Stay out of it, girl!" he says in the same tone.

She sits back as if slapped. Her eyes catch mine and I can see the want in there. She wants to know what I have to say.

"We're staying at Dr. Justice's home," Nancy says, and a flash of gratitude shines from Emily's eyes.

"Doesn't matter where you're staying," the judge says. "Emily will not be seeing you again. Now get out of here before I have you thrown out!"

The door bangs behind us and we walk down the porch stairs and through the gate.

Chapter Four

"Do you mind telling me what that was all about?" Nancy asks as we start down the street from the judge's house.

'Course, I can't tell her about Sarah's tragedy and Emily's shame. "How'd you like being introduced as my wife?" I try to change the subject.

She turns red but doesn't say anything. We walk on, not going too fast.

I hear them before she does. Three sets of running feet coming from behind us. It doesn't seem likely that they're after us, but the judge was real put out with me, and it seems like a good idea to be prudent.

A quick glance shows that I can't see them yet, so I grab Nancy's arm and pull her off the road and between two houses.

"What do you think you're doing?" she queries in a loud voice.

"Shush!" I say, and I guess she can tell I'm serious, on account of she shushes real sudden. The feet keep on coming, and prob'ly she can hear them now too. Three big guys hoof it on by. They are hard-looking and purposeful as they hotfoot it down the road.

"Were they after us?" Nancy asks.

"The judge was mighty put out with me," I respond.

"But he's a judge," she says. "He wouldn't send thugs after us to do us harm."

"I know it doesn't seem likely, but when a man is as worried as I got the judge, you never can tell what he might do. Chances are they weren't after us, but I haven't lived this long by taking chances."

We head back out to the road and walk on toward Doc's place. It's a few minutes before I realize I'm still holding her by the arm and she hasn't said anything about it. 'Course, I let go right away.

As we turn a corner, I see the three men waiting in front of Doc's house.

"I don't suppose you would run away if I told you to," I say to Nancy as we stop a good distance away.

"I would not." She sounds offended. "You forget that we are not in your wild West, Mr. Tee. We are in Boston, where men are civilized and not violent."

I hope she's right, but it doesn't look real promising to me.

"You stay behind me, then," I say, "and I mean it for sure."

She drops back a step or two, but that's about all. It makes me kind of nervous to have a girl to worry about. A man should be able to devote all his attention to any threat. I make sure my coat is open and loose. Feels pretty satisfying to have that Colt parked back there.

Talk or fight, I have to let them make the first move, on account of I don't know all the rules in this big city. Me and Nancy walk on up to them. The shortest one moves forward a little and commences to talk.

"You got any money?" he wants to know. The bigger ones start to sidle off to either side.

"This is a robbery?" Nancy asks, amazed. "In broad daylight?"

He ignores her. "Money," he says. "You got any money?"

It seems to me that they're tryin' to make this look like a robbery gone bad. There doesn't seem to be any good way out of this, and I believe talking will do no good.

My boot knife is a dandy. All of twelve inches long, it's real hefty with a handle covered in leather thong. I can get it out pretty quick when I need to, and it seems like a good time.

The point presses into the skin of the small one's neck before any of them know what's happening. I guess they were expecting no resistance, and everything sort of stops while they take the new situation into account. The guy with the knife touching his neck, his eyes get a little bigger.

I say real soft, "I got one thing to say."

"Wh . . . wh . . . what?" he manages to stammer. That point is getting his attention.

"You got any money?" I ask. He looks surprised.

"Huh?"

"You got any money?" I repeat.

"Yeah," he says. "I got a few dollars."

"Fetch it out," I say. "Only be real careful about how you go about getting it." The other two fellows are edging closer. I glance at the closest one.

"You come one step closer and I'll split his neck for sure," I say.

He appears to think on that some. "You kill

him and the judge'll see that you swing," he finally says.

That is the first I know for sure that the judge is behind them. "If I'm going to swing anyway, there's nothing to stop me from killing both of you," I point out real calm. "So I give you my word that is what I will do."

He's not real bright, a common-enough flaw with some of those big men, and he thinks on that for a good long while. It's like everything is kind of frozen while he makes up his mind. He backs off a step and I know it'll be all right.

His short, mouthy buddy fetches up two dollars and forty-five cents, which he drops in my hand. I allow the money to fall to the street and kick it away. I don't really want his money. I just figure to annoy him some. I guess I must've got the blade too close to him, because a little trickle of red is slowly moving down his neck. He's so stiff it's almost comical as he tries not to move and antagonize me.

I pull the knife away from him.

"Now, git!" I say, and they git, walking slowly away. When they're far enough away to figure they're safe, they turn, and the big, dumb one proves his dumbness once more.

"You'll be sorry you messed with us!" he yells, and then calls me a real nasty name.

Seems like my pistol jumps into my hand before I can stop it, and his eyes open wide as he stares a .45-caliber death in the face.

"I don't put up with talkin' like that around a lady," I say. I'm not talkin' very loud, but he can hear me. "You apologize to the lady, or I'll put a hole in you for sure."

It doesn't take him any time at all to think this over. "I'm truly sorry, ma'am," he says, and his tone says he's telling the truth.

It goes against my grain to draw down on a man and not shoot him, on account of he will sooner or later try to get back at you. Only I sort of gave him my word that if he apologized, I would not.

"You got off lucky for sure," I say, and he appears to be listening to me real hard. "But if I ever see you again, I'll kill you for sure. I am only going to be in town a few days, but if I were you, I'd stay out of sight for at least a week. For sure."

He says nothing, which is the first sign of good sense he has shown. The three of them walk away, and we stand there and watch until they're out of sight. Then Nancy cuts loose on me.

"Mr. Tee," she says, "I thought I told you that it was not permitted to carry a deadly weapon around with you in this city." She doesn't seem at all grateful that I almost just killed a man on account of he swore in front of her. "You cannot kill a man just because he says something you don't like. This city is civilized, Mr. Tee. This city is civilized, and you are not. You will get in trouble, Mr. Tee." She turns and stomps her foot. "You will get in serious trouble. For sure, Mr. Tee," she throws my own words right back at me.

Suddenly, I'm fed up with her. "My name is not Tee," I say to her back, and she stops. "My name is Walker, and I'll thank you to address me that way."

"Why didn't you say something before?" she asks without looking back at me.

"It didn't seem important."

"Humph," she says, and stomps up the porch and into the house. The door slams behind her. I really do not understand women at all.

I stand there a while thinking on it before I notice the curtains are pulled back slightly and James is looking out at me. I feel kind of foolish having him catch me not doing anything, so I walk on up the steps and into the house. He meets me at the door, pulling it open before I can.

"Good morning, Mr. Tee," he says in that snobbish tone of voice.

"My name is Walker," I say.

"Of course, sir," he answers back without batting an eye and then closing the door behind me. "There is coffee in the dining room, Mr. Walker," he goes on. Coffee does sound pretty good.

Doc is sitting there relaxing over a cup of coffee. " 'Morning, John," he says. Somehow, Doc makes things seem normal. Maybe it's the way he talks, so civilized and calm, or maybe it's just that he is so obviously a gentleman. Anyhow, it sure puts the regular back into what has been a kind of unusual day up to now. "Sit and have some breakfast," he says.

"I surely would enjoy sitting with you a spell," I answer back, "but I think I maybe should straighten something out between us."

"What's on your mind?" he wants to know.

"I haven't been all the way honest with you."

"How's that?" He leans back, giving me all his attention.

"My name's not John Tee," I explain. "Well, it really is my name, but it's only part of my name. I am John T. Walker, and I was the man at the stage station who was involved with all the shooting."

His eyebrows go up and down like a couple

of drunk caterpillars. We're both silent for a few seconds while he thinks that over.

"Maybe you'd better sit down and tell me all about it," he finally says.

I guess I need someone to talk to about it, on account of I do just what he says. The only thing I hold back is the part about the map. No sense in tempting people, especially your own friends. Also, I don't say anything about Sarah taking my gun and doing herself in. Sometimes that doesn't set so good with me, so there's no telling how it might set with someone who wasn't there.

"You mean those three brigands attempted to accost you right in front of my own home?"

"Yup."

"I imagine Nancy was quite impressed with the way you handled that precarious situation," he says.

"That's not quite the way I saw it," I'm forced to admit.

James refills my coffee, and it occurs to me I am not exactly sure just how long he has been standing there. Come to think on it, I don't even remember him bringing me the cup in the first place. The man must be good at his job and he should be proud, but he's looking at me like I'm something that slithered out from under the rug. I guess he now knows for sure that I'm a barbarian. He moves off to answer a knock at the side door that Doc uses for his office.

Doc takes a sip of his coffee and looks across the table at me. "That must be the first of my patients for the day," he says. "You just relax and enjoy yourself today, Mr. Walker. We'll see what we can do about your problem at dinner tonight."

"Just Walker, Doc," I say.

"I beg your pardon?"

"Most folks just call me Walker," I explain. "Doesn't quite seem natural to have a Mister in front of it."

"You certainly deserve it," he says with a smile, but that doesn't make any sense to me at all.

After he's gone, I wander into the kitchen, because I can't just sit around and do nothing all day. Macy is busy washing dishes. She seems like a good woman. Keeps herself busy all the time. "Howdy, Macy," I say.

She jumps, splashing water onto the sideboard. "If you are not the quietest man I ever seen!" she says, shaking her head. "Coffee's on the stove," she adds.

I get myself a cup while she works away, bangin' dishes and splashin' water.

"I'm lookin' for something to do," I offer.

"Nothin' needed," she says. "The doctor wouldn't like it if I put you to work."

"I am not a loafer," I say.

"There's a woodpile out back," she says finally, "only I didn't tell you nothing about it."

I feel the muscles in my back tighten as the ax splits the length of wood. I always liked chopping wood. A man has something to measure his work against when he does that. The pile of logs gets smaller while the pile of burning wood gets bigger.

I chop for maybe an hour without stopping, then spike the ax into the block, wipe my forehead on my sleeve, and look around. Nancy is standing on the back porch watching me. I look back but don't say anything. Seems like most everything I say or do sets her off something fierce. We look at each other and the silence drags out. I can hear some little birds chirping and hopping around in the big oak tree behind me.

"The doctor would like to see you if you have a minute," she finally says. "He's in his office with a patient."

"He needs some help, does he?" I ask. I'm trying to be funny. She doesn't smile, but watches me somberly as I walk up and brush past her. "Pardon me, ma'am," I say.

She doesn't say anything, but I can feel her watching me as I go into the house.

I knock easy on the office door.

"Come in," Doc says.

The place smells of alcohol, only it's not the soft kind of alcohol like in a tavern. This smell is hard and somehow clean. Emily is sitting there in a chair next to Doc.

"Hello, Mr. Tee," she says. Her eyes disturb me because they're so much like her dead mother's. Just looking into them takes me back to that awful night, so I watch Doc instead.

"Howdy, ma'am," I say.

Doc leans back in his chair, eyes bright and not saying anything.

"What do you know about my mother?" Emily wants to know.

"I was with her when she died. She died real good, for what it's worth." I think maybe I shouldn't have said that. She looks startled, and I think maybe out East they don't care so much about how a person stands up to dying.

"She was sick?"

"No, ma'am." There's no easy way to say this. "She was shot."

Her eyes open wider. "What?" she cries.

It's hardly possible that she didn't hear me, but I say it again louder: "She was shot, ma'am."

"Who shot her?" she finally asks.

"I'm not quite sure. The bullet came in through the kitchen door and could've come from 'most anyone in the dining room."

"Why would anyone shoot her?" she asks.

"She wasn't shot on purpose. I was working for her at the Mindowan stage station," I begin, and then I tell her like it happened 'cept for the part about Sarah taking my gun and doing what she did. It's hard to tell about that part, and when I'm finished, I feel like I've chopped a whole wagonload of wood.

"Why are you lying to me, Mr. Tee?" Emily asks.

You could hit me with a rifle butt right between the eyes and I couldn't have been more stunned. Nobody in my whole life has ever called me a liar, 'least not to my face. I don't know whether to get mad or to laugh or to walk out.

"Why would you ask that, ma'am?" I say.

"We no longer live in the Middle Ages, Mr. Tee," she says. "I read about the shooting at the Mindowan station in yesterday's paper.

The only survivor was a gunman named Walker. Your name didn't appear in that article anywhere."

"I am Walker, John T. Walker, and I'm not a gunman." This is not going like I figured it would. Not at all. I go on before she can say anything more. "Sarah, your ma, made me promise that I would bring your inheritance." I don't particularly like her sudden change of expression. Her eyes narrow and her pretty face changes into something kind of hard and greedy. I almost wish I didn't have to give her Sarah's money, but I gave my word and I'll keep it. I take the money from my vest pocket and hold it out to her. She takes it right promptly and counts it.

"One hundred and thirty-four dollars?" she asks. "That's all?"

"It's honest money and hard-earned. She also made me promise to take you out to where she lies."

"Out to the frontier?" She tosses her head and her golden hair swishes around her face. "I hardly think so, Mr. Walker."

"That's what she wanted for you."

"She's dead now, Mr. Walker, and it's for me to decide what's best for me."

She gets up, nods to Doc, and leaves. Just

like that. We sit there for a piece, not talking. I don't understand how Sarah could've had a daughter as flighty as Emily.

"Must be her father showing through," I say to Doc.

"She's pretty young," he says, as if that explains everything, and I guess maybe it does. Anyhow, it doesn't look like I'm to be burdened with a young female on my return trip, and in a way it's a relief to me.

"I'll get out of here and let you get back to work," I say. "Unless you need some help with the women."

Doc grins at me. "Yes," he says, "looks like you do real well with the ladies, all right." We both smile.

Macy plops down a piece of apple pie covered with yellow cheese. I can smell the cinnamon, and my fork almost jumps into my hand by itself. The crust flakes away in front of it, and warm apple juice runs out from the filling. It tastes even better than it looks. Nancy is leaning on the sink.

"So you've completed your business," she says. "I suppose you'll be leaving soon."

"Not much around here gets past you women, does it?" I ask around a mouthful of pie.

She has the grace to blush. "I know it's not my business," she says. "I was just making conversation." Then she almost stomps out of the kitchen.

Macy looks down at me with a funny expression. "You sure don't know much about women," she says with a laugh.

Now, a man doesn't like to be told he doesn't know much about anything, only this time I think she may be right. I don't know what it has to do with Nancy, however.

"You're wrong, Macy," I say, thinking mostly about Sarah and Emily. "I clearly don't know *anything at all* about women." 'Long as she keeps feeding me pie, I'll keep agreeing with her.

Much as I like it here in Boston, it's not proper for a man to live off the good will of another man. I know Doc wouldn't mind if I stayed longer, but my chore is done, and although Sarah might not like the result, I can say I did my best if I ever meet her again in the hereafter.

The hereafter is something I haven't really thought much about till lately. Sarah has brought it to mind more than once. Once she passed on, it made me want to know I would be seeing her again someday. It might just be wishing, but it makes me feel easier inside to believe that. Sometimes, I remember lying there with her, holding her close and warm all through that awful night, and the feelings come on so powerful that I must force them back and think on something else lest I mess up my insides for sure.

I lean back from my dinner plate, which is now almost polished since I took my bread and sopped up all the remains. Doc is smiling across the table at me and Nancy is pointedly ignoring me as she waits to clear my place. I get the feeling I might have done something that isn't quite mannerly, only I got no idea what it might be. We are all silent while James pours the coffee. It still feels unnatural to have a grown man take care of me like I was a small child.

"I reckon it's about time for me to leave, Doc," I say. "I do want to thank you for taking good care of me, and I want you to know that I consider you to be a real friend." He may not know it, but that puts him into a mighty small club.

He nods. "I was afraid that would be your intention," he says. "You know, of course, that you are welcome to stay longer if you wish."

"You got Eastern manners and Western hospitality," I say right back.

He grins at me. "I think that's a compliment."

"The best of both worlds, I think," I say back, and I mean it.

I have no wish for a sloppy good-bye, so I excuse myself and head back to my room. James told me that there is a train headed out at nine in the morning, and it's my intention to be on it.

I have only enough money for my ticket back and thirty dollars left over, so I guess I'll be back to punching cows or selling guns again until I can afford a stake to track down that mark on the map. I would like to visit Sarah's grave first, and I guess I can maybe afford to rent a horse for that long.

It doesn't ever take me too long to pack, so I leave things where they are for the night. I strip off my shirt and hang it on the back of the chair. Sleep doesn't come real easy. Seems like I'm always saying good-bye to someone I don't really want to say good-bye to.

I think on the folks living in this house. Doc has James and Nancy and Macy to take care of. And they take care of him too. Comes the end of the day, they know where they'll be and that they will not be by themselves. The lamps will shine yellow from the windows and the house will be there and full of people. Smart people too. Not dumb people who don't know how to talk right or have no proper manners, but people with good breeding and who have been to school. Smart people.

I close my eyes and try to see Sarah's face, only it's fuzzy mostly, 'cept for a flash when I remember her blue eyes. It's getting harder to see her as time fades the hardness of my memory, and even though I know it's my fault, I still feel like she's slowly abandoning me. Pretty soon I'll hardly remember at all what she looked like.

I think that is probably nature's way. A man just can't hurt sharp and hard all the time when he loses someone, on account of it would grow to be too much on him, like a goiter or a tapeworm. It would weaken him and wear him down until he didn't want to put up with it anymore, or until it took over his thoughts so he did something stupid and got himself killed. Nature doesn't want that to happen, so memories of the dead leak away until they can be seen clearly only in an occasional dream.

When I finally get to sleep, I have dreams and they are run through with Sarah and Nancy and Emily all mixed up and confused.

Chapter Five

I snap awake just like I do on the trail sometimes. I lay a hand to my pistol and wait, eyes wide open in the quiet dark, listening hard for whatever it was that woke me. The house is quiet, and it's late, and there's no noise from outside, either.

There's a creak on the floorboard outside my door, and then someone puts a hand to the door handle. The person is trying to be quiet, and that is probably what woke me in the first place. The door starts to open, and I close my eyes to just a crack, so he'll think I'm still sound asleep. I make my breathing regular and steady. The smooth wood of my gun butt feels a comfort to my hand.

For just a second he is framed against the light from the hall, and then he is in the room. He has a club in his hand, and he is not anybody who lives in this house. He comes over to the bed and raises the club.

"Boom!" my .45 says, and the blankets blow up violently from the blast. I can feel hot flecks of powder burn into my bare belly, and whoever he is doubles over in the middle and falls to the floor backward. He lands flat but then pulls himself up double again, trying to get away from the hurt of a lead slug in the belly. I yank my pistol out from under the blankets, thumb back the hammer, and let him have it once more. This time he slams back flat and stays there. The harsh smell of gunpowder fills the room. I can hear my heart pounding hard in my chest.

I slide out and strike a match to the lamp. The yellow light pushes back the dark some, and I pad over and bend down to examine the killer. It's the big, dumb one from earlier in the day. I told him that if I saw him again he was dead, and the slack look on his face tells me I've kept my word.

I hear footsteps coming into the room and figure it's Doc. I only get a quick glimpse of somebody before something smashes into my head and everything goes dark once more.

* * *

It is not really true that you can't see hurt. Hurt is real bright and all full of colored speckles, and it changes just about every time your heart beats. I am looking right at it and feeling it in my head as I slowly come to. Once I open my eyes, most of the white flashes go away, but everything is still a little fuzzy.

Doc and Nancy are sitting in the chairs sort of off in the corner, shadows in their nightclothes. The short guy who tried to rob us in the morning is standing there holding a gun loosely. I want to go take that gun away from Shorty and beat him to death with it, but I feel all weak and dizzy from the knock on the head he gave me. He leans over and looks down on me, and I can see the small scab on his neck where I scratched him with my knife. I waste a moment wishing I had been a little more forceful with him when I had the chance.

"Good morning, Mr. Walker," he says real sneery. "Ain't such a tough man right now, are you?"

I figure he's not really looking for an answer, so I don't say anything. Besides, I'm not quite sure I can talk.

"I'm going to ask you one time," he says. "Where is it?"

I just look at him. He must want the map, which is the only thing I can figure. I don't say nothing.

The little silver gun swings real quick. It smashes me in the left temple and all those flashing white hurts are back once more. I think I hear Doc yell and Nancy scream, but I'm pretty groggy and not certain. As I fight back the lights and hurt, I can feel blood running down the side of my face. Feels like a lot of blood, but I know that head wounds bleed a whole lot even when they're not serious. It might even be a good thing if it makes him think I am hurt worse than I really am.

He's bending over me, and he grabs me under the arms and leans me against the wall. I let my head hang down, and I can hear the dripping of blood from my head to the floor. I struggle to focus my eyes again. He's looking down at me once more.

"Listen, you," he says real mean. "One more minute and I start carving you up a little bit at a time." He's waving my boot knife around. "Where is it?" he asks.

If he thinks I'm just going to lie there while he carves me up, he's not thinking clear. I try to tense up so I can make my move against him, only I'm still as weak as a kitten and I know it's not going to make any kind of difference. A man's gotta try, anyway.

Macy comes in through the door followed by the other man who was with them in the morning. The Quiet One. He, too, is holding a gun.

"She's the only other one I could find," he says to Shorty with the Knife.

Macy looks down at me. "Oh, Dear Lord!" she says, meaning I must look a sight for sure.

"He tell you yet?" the Quiet One asks.

"He was about to," Shorty says with a nasty laugh.

"What do you men want?" Doc asks from the corner. "Money? Drugs?"

"You got money?"

He has attracted Shorty's interest. Good. The longer he talks, the stronger I'm getting.

"At least forty dollars in the house," Doc says back.

Shorty's gun is maybe a .32 caliber. Not real big. He'd have to be pretty lucky to kill a man with the first shot. I am feeling some better, and if I can just get my hands on him, I can take the first one. He's not going to get any second shot.

I'm going to have to try even if I do get shot, on account of what Doc and Nancy and Macy don't know is that these men have got to kill them no matter what else happens. Because they'll be able to identify them.

As for the Quiet One, I will have to keep Shorty between me and him or he will shoot me dead for sure. Maybe I can get Shorty's gun and kill him with it. I must try. There's no other choice for any of us here. It's like it is already written down somewhere, and now the only thing we can do is play it out.

Sometimes, when a man least expects it, God gives him a break. He doesn't necessarily have to deserve it. Breaks just seem to happen every now and then, like they were going to happen in that particular spot at that particular time, and if a man happens to be there, why, he can take advantage of it or not, as he sees fit.

Shorty flips my knife into the floor by my left knee. I don't know if he did it on purpose or if he was trying to pin my leg to the floor. But my knife thuds into the floor and quivers there right next to my leg. For sure, he doesn't expect that I can get anywhere near it, on account of he thinks I'm hurt bad.

"Missed," he says to his partner, and looks toward him for just a second. I bend forward and go for that knife as quick as I can. Something is dreadfully wrong with my head, for it seems like I am moving real slow. Shorty turns back to me, takes in what I'm trying, and raises that pretty little gun toward me.

I feel the familiar haft in my hands, and I use that simple wrist flip that Cherokee taught me. It doesn't take a whole lot of motion to put a powerful force behind a throw that way, and the knife thumps into Shorty's belly clean up to the hilt at about the same time that his gun goes off. On account of I am bent forward, I feel the heavy hammer of the bullet going down my back, and even though I see the Quiet One turning his gun on me, I suddenly don't have any more strength left in me.

Shorty has an awful expression on his face, kind of pasty and white. My knife must have hit something real vital, because blood is pouring out and staining his shirt and trousers already. Then his knees fold up and he falls across my legs. He's lying on me and I can tell he's holding himself real stiff, prob'ly because it must hurt him whenever he moves any.

I realize I am leaning back against the wall, prob'ly where I wound up after Shorty's bullet got done with me. The little silver gun is lyin' there only a few inches from my hand, but I've got no strength left to reach for it. I must try, though. If I don't, the Quiet One is going to kill everyone for sure. Me, I figure I'm already done for, so I put my mind on reachin' for that gun and pay no mind to the fact that he's going to shoot me before I can get to it.

The blast of a .45 fills the room, and I would know the sound of that gun anywhere. It is *my* gun, and I can see James standing there by the door thumbing back the hammer for another shot. The Quiet One is sitting on the floor with his legs splayed out in front of him, a real surprised expression on his face.

"Take that, you evil man," I hear James say, and bad hurt as I am, I want to laugh on account of I never heard anybody who was mad talk so proper. My .45 booms again and the Quiet One is flat on his back, staring at the ceiling and no longer concerned with the goings-on.

I look up and see Nancy looking me right in the eyes. Her eyes are brown and she looks concerned. I want to tell her that she doesn't have anything to worry about anymore, only I can't seem to make the words come out. Shorty suddenly relaxes with a sigh, and it appears to me like I'm going to be right behind him. I'm looking Nancy right in the eye as things start to go dark.

A man could die lookin' at lots worse things than her, and it's almost like her eyes draw me in until I can't see anything else. And then I can't see them anymore, either.

Chapter Six

Funny dreams. Faces. Of people long dead. Of Sarah. Of Nancy and Doc. Of James and Macy and Emily. All blurred together and mixed up. Sometimes talking, sometimes not. Faces of men I killed and men who were trying to kill me. Shorty and the Quiet One and the Big Dumb One. And Nancy again. And Nancy again. Being dead isn't so bad after all. I try to roll over.

Pain. Hot and real angry tears roll down my cheeks. My eyes snap open but I don't move any.

That's one of the things you learn to do in wild country. When you wake up, make sure of where you are and what's going on before you move. Might be a bear in camp. Or a snake on your belly. You stay alive only by being careful. All the time.

I'm looking square at Nancy. She's slumped in a chair, eyes closed, covered with a quilt. She looks all worn out. The quilt rises and falls with her breathing.

I hear footsteps in the hall, and it all comes flooding back to me—the fighting and the killing.

The door opens and I am looking Doc right in the eye. He smiles like he's surprised, and comes on in. The floor creaks under his step, and Nancy's eyes pop open.

"Hello, Walker," Doc says, and Nancy looks over at me. Her eyes are tired with the deep, deep weariness that tears a body down. I wonder how long she has been sitting there and watching over me. She brightens up some when she sees me looking back at her.

"Hi, Walker," she says softly.

I try to nod at her, but it proves to be a big mistake. The room swims and my head pounds with each beat of my heart.

" 'Mornin', Miss Nancy," I say.

"Bet your head hurts, huh?" Doc asks. I look at him as best I can. "You have a concussion," he explains. "Lucky you aren't dead, actually. When he hit you in the temple with that gun, I thought you were done for."

"It got my attention," I admit. My mouth is

as dry as flour. Nancy pours a glass of water from the pitcher and comes over to me. I want it something awful, but I'm not quite sure I can sit up. To my surprise, she slides her arm under me and raises me up off the pillow.

I sip at the water and feel how soft and firm her arm is underneath me. I almost forget about the dizziness. She holds me there, glass to my lips, until the entire glass is empty. I still don't feel like I got enough wet in me, but she eases me back onto the pillow and puts one hand on my brow.

I'm not used to young women being so nice to me, and her hand is so soft and warm on my forehead that I can't seem to think of anything else. Must be some gift women have, so that when a man's sick, they can just lay hands on him here and there and he feels better.

"How bad am I shot?" I ask Doc.

"It's fortunate you were leaning forward at the time," he explains. "The bullet sort of slid down your ribs but never did get in to anything vital. Broke two of them, though."

"Always favored a .45 myself."

"Certainly would've changed the outcome," he agrees.

"I thought you were dead," Nancy says, and her voice catches.

Huh? I didn't even think she liked me at all! Guess all a man has to do to get a woman's attention is to get hisself shot. "You'd better get some rest," she goes on.

"I'll do that, ma'am, for sure," I say. "Only I'd surely appreciate another glass of that water and maybe some hotcakes and bacon and coffee if Macy doesn't mind."

Doc grins at Nancy. "I think he's going to be all right," he says.

Her eyes fill and she looks like she might cry. I'll never understand women as long as I am alive.

"I'll go arrange for some food," Doc says, and away he goes.

Nancy fills the glass again and lifts me up. I sip away at the glass and look up at her. Tears are running down her cheeks, but she's not making any noise at all. I am looking into her eyes and drinking, and once again they sort of swallow me up and then fade away. 'Least, I'm not thirsty anymore.

The sound of the door opening wakes me up. It is dark outside, the room yellow with lamplight. James comes in carrying a tray.

"Howdy, James," I say. My voice doesn't quite sound right. Prob'ly need to wet it some.

"Hello, Mr. Walker," he says. He slides his arm behind me as gently as a girl and props me up on a pillow. It makes me woozy for a short minute.

"Not Mr. Walker," I explain. "Just Walker."

He nods while I take a sip of water. "Very well," he says. "How do you feel?"

"Like I've been beat on with rocks."

He doesn't smile. Come to think on it, I have never seen him smile. He uncovers some steak and eggs, and all of a sudden I'm starved. He carves off a piece, spears it with a fork, and holds it up to my mouth.

Now, it isn't right for a man to feed another man who can do it for himself, so I take the fork away. I may be weak and kind of trembly, but I'm no invalid. I start to chew, and he heads for the door, then stops and turns to me.

"Do you ever get used to it?" he wants to know.

I know what he is talking about right away. "No," I say. "You kill because you must and there's no other choice, and that helps, but the faces will keep coming back to mind, mostly at night. You'll wonder about their family and what they must think of you, but remember that it's better that *their* family is grieving and not yours." I pause and he nods, listening hard. I go on. "That varmint was needful of killing, and you did good when you did it. You did it right too. I was taught that you always shoot them twice, so they can't recover and come after you when you're not expecting it."

"It was so violent, and it happened quicker than I ever imagined."

"It's always that way. Life isn't always as pretty as it's made out to be."

"You're right about that, Walker," he says, and goes out the door. Before he even gets it closed Nancy comes in.

She has changed clothes since last I saw her, and she must've got some sleep too, 'cause she doesn't look so tired anymore. I'm glad to see her, and that particular emotion about her surprises me. She comes over, takes the fork, and starts to feed me like I'm an infant. I'm tired clean through and it doesn't seem so bad to be fed by a woman. Matter of fact, it's pretty nice.

It takes me a full week before I can get out of bed and get dressed. Macy has washed my clothes, and they're as clean-smelling and soft as can be when I finally pull them on. For a minute I don't think I'm going to be able to manage my boots, but I grit my teeth and bend over and pull them on. I sling my gun belt around me, check my Colt, shuck and replace the four empties. I feel dressed for the first time since I got here.

The stairs are a caution, but I manage. Nobody is in the dining room so I head for the kitchen. It smells of coffee and bacon.

Macy looks right concerned when I come in, but I wave her off and go sit down at the table. She plunks a cup of coffee down in front of me before I can say anything.

" 'Mornin', Mr. Walker," she says. "You sure you should be up and around yet?"

"Feel fine, Macy," I say, only I must admit I'm weak. It isn't but a few minutes before she puts a plate of bacon and eggs and potatoes down in front of me and I commence to eat. Seems like I got the appetite of a horse lately. Got to eat to build back my strength, I guess.

So far nobody has asked me what those men were after, but I don't doubt they're all as curious as can be. Doc told me a lawman showed up and said the judge claimed he had fired all three men earlier in the day when they told him about trying to hold up Nancy and me. I got my doubts about the good judge, and that's for sure.

Nancy comes in, takes one look at me, and commences to bawl me out for being out of bed. The thought of being back in that bed doesn't appeal to me at all, and I guess my patience is wore thin, because I let her nag for a while and then I shout, "Enough!" She shuts up like she's been smacked and begins to pick at her breakfast like a sullen child. Of course, I feel real bad right away, because she has been doing nothing but helping me for the last week and I got no cause to snap at her.

Women are experts at making a man feel like a heel. It doesn't take them hardly any effort at all, and you'd think men would get wise to it, only it works every time. It doesn't make sense. Here she was nagging away at me, and I feel like I ought to apologize to *her*. I'm not going to do it, though.

We eat in some almighty quiet until Doc comes in.

" 'Morning, Walker."

" 'Morning, Doc."

"I'll eat in here this morning, Macy," he says, and plops down on a chair. He studies on me like a doctor for a minute. "Feels good to be out of bed, doesn't it?" he finally says.

"Yes, it does," I answer around a mouthful of potatoes. I take a sip of coffee and lean back. "They were after a map, I think," I explain, getting their attention for sure. "I found it on the stranger who was at the center of all the trouble at the stage station." Another sip. "I have no idea what it leads a man to, and I also have no idea what it says on it." I look at Nancy, trying not to look shamed on account of I cannot read writing. "Seems that I've spent so much of my life just trying to stay alive that I never had time to learn how to read," I explain to her. I cannot read her expression.

"The newspaper mentioned that he might have had a map," Doc says.

I am amazed. I absolutely have got to learn to read. "How could they know about the map?" I ask.

"Some other men were hunting for him too," Doc explains. "Pinkertons."

"Pinkertons?" They are some of the best manhunters in the land. 'Most always, they're on the side of the law. "Why would they want the map?"

"Supposed to lead to a buried cache of gold,"

Doc says. "A group of Spaniards had mined it and were taking it out of the mountains on two pack mules when they were discovered by Indians. They buried the gold and made the map before they were slaughtered."

"Who does the gold really belong to?" I ask.

"The first one who finds it, I guess," he comes back.

I sit back and sip at my coffee. I certainly have a lot to ponder on. Of course, I have heard lots of gold stories before, and they always turned out to be untruths. There's something about gold, though, the way it makes a man want for things he never had any need of before.

"It appears to me that since that story is out, I might have a whole bunch of folks looking for me," I observe. "Might be those three were just the first to find out about the map." Nancy looks real distressed all of a sudden. Can't say as I blame her, since being around me is prob'ly not all that healthy right now.

"I'd say that's a reasonable assumption," Doc agrees.

"I got to get out of here."

"I don't think anybody will bother you while you're here."

"Maybe you forgot we had to kill three people

in this house only a week ago," I say. "More are sure to come. To tell the truth, I don't feel real comfortable here in the city. I need to get back to the country, where I'm more at home. At least there I'll have an even chance." 'Course, that's prob'ly what that stranger at the station thought before all those hardcases showed up and shot him full of holes.

"You can't go alone," Doc says.

"I cannot be watching out for somebody else," I say right back.

"You misunderstand. You're going to require a lot of sleep for at least another week. You need someone to watch over you."

"Only living people in the whole world I trust are in this house," I say. "And, no offense, but I don't believe that any of you are suitable to stand guard over me."

"I am," James says from over by the door.

I must be getting old, on account of I never heard him come in. Everybody turns and contemplates James for a long minute. I ponder him in my mind. He's right. He is the only one I can trust to watch over me, on account of he has already proved he can pull a trigger when he has to. I can see that it doesn't sit real well with Doc, although Nancy nods and seems satisfied.

"You?" Doc asks him. "Out West?"

"Doc," I butt in, "if he's willing to go and you are willing to let him go, he's more than enough man for me."

James looks at me kind of surprised, but then his normal flat expression takes over again.

Doc thinks on it for a minute. "I can't see any way around it," he says. He gives a little chuckle. "You'll be the first cowboy with his own servant."

I don't much like the sound of that, but I let it ride on account of Doc is my friend.

"James and I will go where that map leads," I say. "And once we have that all settled, there'll be no reason for all those people to hunt me anymore."

And it's settled just that quick. Since the next train leaves at three o'clock tomorrow afternoon, all in the house are suddenly busy getting us ready for the trip. 'Cept for me. I spend most of the day in bed. The quicker I heal up, the better it'll be for James and me.

When I wake up, it's getting dark, and James comes into my room and lights the lamps. He is wearing plain clothes like mine, and he has a new gun belt with shiny new cartridges in all the loops. The holster holds a brand-new blue steel Colt .45, and he looks so uncomfortable that he borders on miserable. I have to laugh, which doesn't help his attitude any.

"You find this apparel amusing?" he wants to know.

"It's not the outfit," I explain. "It's how miserable you look wearing it."

"I must admit I feel somewhat ludicrous."

"If ludicrous means the same as foolish, you got nothing to worry about," I say right back. "Once those clothes get a little wear, you'll be taken for a dangerous man for sure." He will too, on account of he's so serious all the time. It has been my experience that most folks don't fool with men who are serious all the time.

Dinner is great. Macy outdoes herself with the roast beef and potatoes and ice cream, but the mood is kind of held back because we all know we're going to be apart for a long time starting tomorrow. Every time I look up, Nancy is looking at me kind of unusual, and I have no idea what that expression means on a woman.

We sit up late, gathered round in the yellow of the lamps, sometimes talking, sometimes just quiet. I like these people and I'll surely feel their not being around me anymore.

James doesn't say much at all, and I can't

say as I blame him any. It takes a lot of man to up and leave everything he's familiar with to set off for the unknown just to help a friend. There's certainly a lot more to James than I ever suspected when I first arrived. Just goes to show that you cannot tell about a man by what he first appears to be.

Nancy and Doc insist on coming to the station with us even though we tell them they don't have to. Nancy sits next to me in the carriage, and she seems closer than she really has to be, but I don't mind a bit. The wheels rumble on the bricks and it's a long, quiet ride in the carriage, what with each of us wrapped up in his and her own thoughts. Nancy keeps watching me, and I feel bad at leaving her behind, which surprises me some, on account of I didn't think we liked each other at all.

Just before we get on the train, Doc shakes my hand and shakes James's hand too. Nancy comes over to me and, for the love of Mike, she reaches up and gives me a long hug, right there in front of everybody.

"You be careful, Walker," she says to me real soft but firm.

I am mighty surprised for sure. "Good-bye, Nancy," I say back. "I'll take good care of James."

She lets go and steps back, and then James and I get on the train. When I look out the window, she is standing there with tears running down her face. It is plain she's going to miss James something awful. She doesn't have to worry much. I will keep him from harm the best I can. I must admit I feel no pleasure at leaving them behind, and I stare out the window and watch the country go by.

Chapter Seven

I have no doubt that James and I are being followed. There's bound to be someone who's willing to take a chance on taking us down and getting that map for himself. I don't really expect that anyone will try anything on the train, on account of he'd have too much trouble, what with the other passengers and all. So I sleep as many hours as I can, leaving James to sit there and watch the country change into the West once more.

The trip takes only three days this time. Seems like maybe the railroad is starting to get itself in order. Glad I don't own a stage line, and that's for sure. When we get off, I must admit I'm glad to be done with trains for a while. I am rump-weary and ready for a good night of sleep on something that isn't bouncing me all over. James confesses he is tired too, so we head over to the hotel. We have a tolerable steak dinner, although it is nothing like one of Macy's meals, and lock ourselves in our room for the night. I show James how to wedge a chair under the doorknob so nobody can get in, and we both sleep until morning.

James is a mystery to me, mostly. He's quiet and steady, and doesn't hardly ever seem to run down. He says Doc gave him enough money so we could get ourselves outfitted. I don't like that much, but I cannot see any way around it right now, so I told him to keep careful account of what we spend so I can pay Doc back someday. 'Course, if we do hit it big, Doc is entitled to a full share as far as I'm concerned.

Comes the dawn and I show James the map for the first time. He ponders over the writing for a while.

"It's in Spanish," he says. "The hill on the left is called Buffalo Head. They buried the gold under a dead mule a hundred and fifty paces east of a small spring."

"I know the place, on account of I used to hunt around there sometimes," I say. "Spring is dried up now, and they call the hill Buff Butte, but I recollect seeing the mule's skull half buried in the ground. Takes three days' ride from the station."

We buy two good horses and a packhorse too. James would have bought the first horse the hostler brought out, so it's a good thing that I'm with him to point out the bad features. We buy supplies and, best of all, two repeating Winchesters and plenty of ammunition. James says he can already shoot a rifle pretty fair, so I'll work on his handgun with him when we get out on the trail.

Sooner we get out of town, the happier I'll be. I feel like we're being watched all the time, and we prob'ly are, only I can't pick out who it is with so many people around. Out on the trail, though, they'll be easier to spot.

It's midafternoon before we're ready, and we tie up in front of the hotel and go in for one last meal that we won't have to cook ourselves. Later, with full bellies, we swing into the saddle, and it sure is nice to hear the familiar squeak of leather and to feel a solid horse beneath me once more. My mind says everyone is watching us as we ride out of town, and I can still feel their eyes long after the town falls back over the horizon.

The sun is just starting to set when we pause on the ridge overlooking the Mindowan stage station. There's smoke rising from the chimney and yellow lantern light showing clear at the windows. It's passing strange to see life where there was so much death only a month ago. We ride on down from the high ground into the dusk. I ride around to the graves and James follows right along. It's getting dark, but not so black I can't see the graves and markers. Sarah's is right in front of me, and the darkness has filled in the letters that are carved there, but I can still see them clearly in my mind.

It is hard to believe that under that dry dirt lies the pretty, blue-eyed lady who would have loved me and shared the rest of my life. She was so alive, but under there she's just an empty body, and the alive part of her has leaked out and gone away. I wonder where. It's hard for me to imagine what life could have been like if that stray bullet had gone just a little bit farther right and missed her altogether.

I kick my horse into motion and we walk around to the hitching rail in front. James follows along behind. Sometimes, even when he has someone with him, a man can feel all alone.

Sarah is much on my mind as I walk through that familiar front door. The room doesn't look much different, but the people do. There are six hard men eating in pairs at various tables around the room. My table—I can't help calling it that—is empty, and James and I go sit there sort of side by side, each with his back to the wall. James learns fast.

Them six men look us over when we arrive, but appear to pay us no mind once they decide we're no threat to them. I can see a couple of the tables have holes in them from the last time I ate in here.

A short, wrinkled-up old man shuffles out of the kitchen and over to us.

"What'll it be, gents?" he wants to know. His voice is faint and reedy with lots of breath in it, and I believe there may be something amiss in his lungs.

"Dinner," I say. "And coffee."

"Be forty cents," he says right back. "Each."

He's not sure we have the money, I think, so I lay a dollar on the table and he looks satisfied and heads back for the kitchen. A few minutes later, the familiar metal plates clank as he sets them down on the rough wood in front of us. Dinner is beans and bacon, and I got to say that the food quality has gone down some from the last person who ran this place. He doesn't go right back to the kitchen this time.

"You know," the old guy says, "you're settin' right where he did."

"Who?" I ask.

"Walker, o'course," he goes on. "From right there he kilt all them men. For an extra dime I'll tell you all about it. I was here, you know."

"No, thanks," I reply. I am slightly amused. Who'd have ever thought I'd be so famous someday that other men would lie about me.

"It's worth the dime," he whines. "I'll even show you the bed where he shot the woman he loved. She used to run this place, you know."

Anger is not a good thing. It makes a man do harsh things that he wouldn't do otherwise. It throws away caution and makes the future seem not so important as the present. You can almost see anger. It is a red cloud that storms up just behind where you can see and makes thinking stop and harsh action happen.

The table smashes to the floor as I jump to my feet, and I don't remember how my gun got in my hand and pointed at his face, but it's cocked and my finger is tight on the trigger. His eyes are open so wide it's a wonder they don't fall plumb out of his head and into his open mouth.

"Walker!" James calls. "Walker, don't!"

The old man hears my name, and it's like all the strength leaves his knees and he slowly sags to the floor. My gun barrel follows him down, and it's plain to see I've scared him nigh on to death, and me too. I've never been so mad in my life, but it's wearing off and I'm starting to think again.

To their credit, nobody else in the room is moving nary a muscle. James is standing beside me with his hand on his gun, watching for any happenings in the room.

"I think we're about finished here, don't you?" he asks without lookin' at me.

"I would say so," I agree softly. I'm not too proud of what I just did, but I wasn't going to apologize to anybody, 'least not in my present mood. I let my hammer down and slide my gun back in the holster. The old man closes his eyes and breathes a big sigh. James and I are not bothered as we head out the door. In fact, nobody in the room moves so much as a muscle until we're gone.

We mount and ride off into the dark. I am cussing myself something awful, and I deserve every word of it. Closest I ever came to killing an innocent man, and it has scared me some. Maybe they're right, and I've become as bad as they make me out to be. Only, I don't think so. Human life is something special, something to be cherished and preserved unless it's them or me, and I still believe that.

So the lie is out about the way Sarah died. I should have expected it, since it could have looked that way to anyone who wasn't there but just read the signs. It saddens me some. The way of her dying was a private thing, a special thing between me and her, and now it's being put on display for other folks' unholy entertainment. I don't like it, not even a little bit.

We ride up the ridge, James putting his trust in me to find the way in the dark. I used to hunt here quite a lot, and it has always been my practice to take note of likely campsites when I'm out. I don't like riding in the dark much, and my horse doesn't like it much either, but in three hours we are at the spot I have in mind.

It's a small cavelike depression in the cliff face that's surrounded by big rocks that provide plenty of cover. I hobble the horses and set up the camp on account of James doesn't have any idea what's to be done. Before too long I have a fire going and coffee cooking. I slice some bacon and throw some beans in a pot of water.

"Supper will be ready shortly," I tell him. "How do you like being waited on by somebody else for a change?"

"I think I could get used to it," he says. To his credit, he hasn't asked me anything about the way Sarah died. In fact, he hasn't said a single word since we left the station. I find I'm liking this quiet man more and more.

After we eat and I've cleaned the dishes, we sit around the fire and sip at our coffee. James looks done in, and I guess that for an indoor man, all this outdoors can be tiring for the first few days. I take a sip of coffee and commence to telling him what I think he should know.

"She was gut-shot," I say. He looks at me, but doesn't say anything. I go on. "Being gut-shot is about the worst way to die there is. Awful painful and takes a long time. There's no dignity in it after the real pain starts."

"You don't have to talk about it," he says.

"I want you to know," I say right back. "Because the full truth is less hurtful than what a body can dream up. Besides, you have a right to know something that important about the man you're trusting your life to." He doesn't say anything.

"She asked me to do it," I go on. The fire cracks softly and a small spike of sparks raises into the dark, winking out before they get too high. "I was fond of her and couldn't help her in any other way, but still I couldn't do it. She took my gun, and when I was out of the room, she shot herself. Every night since, I've asked myself if I really knew she'd taken my gun and if I left it with her on purpose or not." I sigh. "I don't feel good about it." There, it's said.

He crawls into his bedroll and turns from the fire. He's a hard man to read sometimes.

"You know, Walker," he says into the dark, "you think you are a crude man, and maybe you are, but you are a man of principles, and they are good principles. I think you are a good man, Nancy thinks you are a good man, and so do Dr. Justice and Macy. We can't all be wrong."

As is usual when I can't think of what to say, I don't say anything. Before long, I can tell from his regular breathing he is asleep. I trust the horses to let us know if we get any company, so I figure on sleeping too. But I have lots to think on, and it takes me a lot longer to drop off than it did James.

I didn't realize how noisy Boston was at night compared to what I'm used to. Now I can almost hear the quiet, almost feel my ears stretching open to take it all in. The usual night-insect sounds put a man's mind at ease no matter how trying the circumstances, and I could swear I hear a woman's sweet voice singing away off in the distance.

Chapter Eight

The sun rises red and bloody, a bad sign sometimes. James is an early riser too, and we have eaten and cleaned camp before seven. He's surprised when I let the fire go out and still don't show any signs of wanting to leave. As he sits with me, I can tell he wants to know what I have in mind, only he dares not ask. To his credit, it doesn't take him too long to figure it out.

"We will stay here for a while and see how many are on our trail," he says.

I nod, and we sit in silence for maybe a half hour.

"I heard a woman singing last night," he says.

I look at him, surprised. "Me too. But I thought it was my imagination."

I ponder on that while we watch our back trail. I cannot imagine what a woman would be doing out here.

It isn't too long before we see four riders coming along. They stop a goodly distance out and look up at the rocks where we lay. I can tell they don't like the situation at all, and I don't blame them any. If I was really the gunman they all make me out to be, I could easily shoot them down if they keep on coming. Be a simple matter to let them get in rifle range and then ambush them. I take four rifle shells and stand them on the rock. When they find them, they'll know I could have killed them had I wanted to. Maybe that will turn them back.

James smiles when he sees what I did, and we mount up and head out again. We haven't gone too far before we come upon a campsite that must be where the woman was we heard singing. There were two of them, and they pulled out about an hour before we got there, headed west, same as us. This desolate country seems awful crowded all of a sudden.

We catch up with them just before noon. They have spotted us and are standing their horses, waiting. They are both Mexican, the woman no more than a girl and the man a big fellow with a clean gun.

"*Buenos días,*" she says.

"Howdy, ma'am," I come right back. "We weren't following you." I want to get that out of the way. "Just going in the same direction." She smiles friendly-like, but the man doesn't say anything and stays back where he can watch us both.

"I am Conchita Luis," she says. "And this is Manuel Daga."

"Charmed, Miss Luis," James says with his elegant voice, and I can see she's somewhat taken aback by him. "We were just planning to stop for a noonday repast," he goes on. "Perhaps you would care to join us?"

This is all news to me. Actually, I figured on riding hard all day with maybe some jerky in the saddle.

"Why, I'd love to, Mr. . . . ?"

"Dagget," he says. "James Dagget, recently of Boston." It's the first I knew he had a last name. "This is my friend, Mr. John T. Walker," he introduces me.

"Ma'am," I say and touch my hat. Miss Luis and her man look at each other at the mention of my name. It appears they may have heard about me.

"We'd be happy to lunch with you," she replies, and I can tell that her man isn't real pleased with this, but he doesn't say anything. I don't blame him a bit. If she was under my care, I'd be mighty careful of strangers too.

"I believe we can find a better spot to rest if we ride on a piece," I suggest.

"Anywhere you suggest, Mr. Walker," she says real cheerful, and I almost smile at the sourness of her man's expression. He doesn't like us at all, I'm thinking.

In another thirty minutes we come across a good spot with plenty of cover for us and none for anybody who's coming from behind. Daga studies my choice of campsites, and he nods slightly in approval. Still, he dismounts last, and as he helps get the fire going, he's real careful not to let either of us get behind him. I think I could like him, on account of we seem to have a way of thinking in common.

James breaks out some pans and commences to cooking. Another surprise from him. I never figured he knew his way around a cooking fire, but I can tell real shortly that he knows what he's doing.

"Have you ever been to Boston, Miss Luis?" he asks. "It's quite an attractive metropolis, but the scenery pales before this." He points to the views all around us.

"Never to Boston, Mr. Dagget," she says. "Have you ever been to Mexico?"

"Never," he comes back. "But I would very much like to visit there someday."

"Should you ever come to Juarez, you would be welcome at our hacienda," she says shyly.

"I will look forward to that," he says.

I am truly amazed. What happened to the silent James I was so used to? Here he's almost babbling to a young Mexican woman, and she has already invited him home to meet her folks. I take another look at her.

She is pretty and short, with a small nose and full, pouty lips. Her shiny black hair is done up in a tight bun and she looks very elegant and very female in her full riding skirt and bangled vest. She only comes up to my shoulders, but in women, size doesn't matter much, and the tiny ones can be just as powerful as the tall ones. It just depends on the man they get to, and she has certainly got to James Dagget. I can tell easily, and find it amusing. When I look over at Daga, I can tell he doesn't find it amusing at all. Something about her seems familiar, but I'm sure I've never seen her before.

James comes up with some hash that's better than any I've ever eaten before. All the while, he and she are talking and appreciating each other enough to make a man smile. Daga may not like the way things are going between them, but I notice that it doesn't hurt his appetite any. James and Miss Luis don't hardly eat anything at all, so Daga and I are forced to finish up the food, which doesn't really bother either of us.

"Would you care to ride with us a ways?" Miss Luis asks, and that stops Daga in midchew. I think he was hoping we would just disappear.

"We'd love to," James says without even looking at me. I seem to have lost control of this situation altogether.

I'm not so sure it's a good idea to take them along when we do not know what we're riding into, but I suppose it can't hurt anything for the rest of the day. Might even give me a chance to do some scouting around without worrying about James being alone in the wilderness.

So we break camp and mount up. In what is almost a footrace, James beats Daga over to help Miss Luis get up on her horse. James puts his hands on her waist and helps her to her saddle while Daga practically bristles beside him just like a mean old dog. I can almost hear him growl.

"Thank you, Mr. Dagget," she says, and smiles down on him bright enough to light the night sky. James is almost struck down by her, plain as day. Been a long time since I have seen a grown man act like an addled schoolboy. Miss Luis notices that Daga is hovering around just beside her.

"Mount up, Manuel," she says, kind of surprised. "It is not like you to lag behind."

The expression on his face is pure nasty cussedness. No doubt he would like to shoot the both of us. Prob'ly like to shoot our horses, our kin, and all our friends while he's at it. He grabs his saddle horn and swings up to his seat. I can't help myself and I give him a great big smile. I am enjoying all this a whole lot. His expression back to me has no joy in it at all, and that adds some to my urge to laugh.

We head out, riding west into the sun for most of the afternoon. James and Miss Luis stay together, with me leading and Daga bringing up the rear, no doubt planning our immediate and awful demise. They are talking for the entire afternoon, and I got to admit I wouldn't mind a little of the quiet James back again, just to give my ears a rest. I pick a campsite early, on account of the sun is getting lower and more direct into our eyes as the day wears on. Daga approves of my choice, and James and Miss Luis couldn't care less about where we camped as long as they are together.

They remind me of me back when Lilly Lipman was the most important thing in my life. I was maybe fourteen, and the first time I saw her she had such a powerful effect on me I thought I was sick for sure. When I straightened out in my mind that it was want for her that made me feel that way, it messed me up something fierce. I couldn't talk to her in any way, shape, or form. I mean, here was this girl who I loved so bad, and whenever she was around, I got tongue-tied and was scared to say anything at all.

I finally got up enough nerve to ask her to meet me at the Saturday dance. I can still remember the terror I felt at going up to this slip of a girl and asking her to meet me. I stammered and could tell my face was beet-red, and sweat broke out over my entire body.

She smiled at me like I was funny, tossed her hair, and said, "Certainly not." It was just what I'd expected, but I was a broken man right there. Girls have no idea how bad they can hurt a man with just a little contempt.

'Course, love has no pride, so I would've tried again, only that business with Mr. Devroe happened and her brother was one of them that I killed.

I've been sort of scared of women ever since then, although I sure wouldn't tell that to anybody. I mean, she was so powerful that I had no control over myself, and it scared me some. With Sarah it would have been different, on account of she found something in me that she must have liked. She made me feel warm and wanted, and sometimes at night I still bring out that feeling and think maybe I'm not such a bad man after all.

Emily kind of reminded me of Lilly. It wouldn't be above her to use a man all up and then hurt him and throw him down. She sure was pretty, though, and would make a fine woman if she was only more like Nancy. Nancy seemed more like Sarah than Emily ever would. Maybe it's like Doc said, and Emily is just too young. Maybe it takes age before a woman realizes the worth of a man. If so, I fear James is riding for a hard fall, because Miss Luis cannot be much over eighteen.

'Course, Nancy is not very old either, but she acts old, prob'ly on account of her father getting killed when she was young. Nancy seems to be coming into my thoughts an awful lot lately, like when we're riding and there's not any talking going on. I don't have any trouble remembering her face with its cute little nose, and how wrinkled up and funny it looks when she gets angry. I can see her easy when she stamps her foot and puts her little fists on her hips like she did when I spilled the pudding that time.

She would make a man a fine wife, what with her learning and her spunk. I can easily remember her soft arm under my head and the way she took care of me when I was hurt. I think that maybe she has a soft side that would surprise a man and sort of overwhelm him if he ever gave her a chance. I'm kind of surprised that I'd like to give her that chance. 'Course, she wouldn't want anything to do with me, I expect, on account of she thinks I'm a barbarian. Compared to her, I guess I am.

Don't know when I'll see her again, if ever. Right now, I am a day's ride plus three or four days on a train away from her. Strange way for me to think about distance, and that's for sure.

Daga started the fire and didn't say anything as he watched me ride out. James was getting the cooking stuff out, so I guess I'll be doing no more cooking while he's along. He must not have been too proud of my beans last night.

It's pretty nice to be off on my own, even if it's only for an hour or so. It's a wonder those two are not all talked out, what with gabbing all afternoon. Prob'ly be hoarse by tomorrow, I figure.

'Course, Daga makes up for them on account of he hasn't spoken a word all day long 'cept for a few sentences in Spanish to Miss Luis. I don't even know if he can talk English, but he can sure look annoyed in any language.

There's nobody behind us that I can see, but they're out there somewhere, on account of I can *feel* them. They are prob'ly doing the same as I would, waiting until we've got where we're going before they make a move. Prob'ly won't be any trouble at all until day after tomorrow.

Dinner is beans and bacon again, and I got to admit they don't taste anything like mine at all. They are better than all right, an opinion obviously shared by Daga. I figure that if he was to stay with us for another week, he'd weigh in about the same as my horse, the way he eats. Coffee is fine too.

"Mr. Walker," Miss Luis asks as we sit around the fire, "would you be the same Mr.

Walker who was involved in the shooting at the stage station?"

"I would be him, ma'am," I admit.

"Then you're the man I have come so far to see," she says right back.

Huh? What could she possibly want with me? I just raise an eyebrow but don't say anything, on account of I can't think of anything to say.

"My brother was there also," she says softly.

I look at her hard. Sure enough, that's why she looked kind of familiar to me. Her brother must have been the Mexican with the missing finger.

"Your brother have part of a finger missing?" I ask. She nods. "He was there, then," I say. "He was killed for nothing he did, as far as I know. He was just eating supper with a friend when those bandits came in and all the shooting started. He was shot twice, but he got in a few good licks before he died." There had been three used shells in his gun, as I recollect. She seems to be taking it pretty well. "I only met him that day, but he struck me as a man to cross the river with," I finish.

"He was just in the wrong place at the wrong time?" she says softly.

"Yes, ma'am. That's about the size of it."

"What a stupid way to die."

"Wasn't anybody died real smart that day, Miss Luis," I reply, thinkin' of Sarah especially.

"The man at the station told me how it happened," she says. "He said he was there."

"He's a liar, ma'am."

"I rather suspected as much. Can you please tell me about my brother, about what really happened?"

And so I do. I start from when her brother and the dude and the kid showed up, and I take her right on through the shooting and dying. I don't tell her about her brother gurgling and choking on the table. She doesn't need to know about that.

"We buried him good and proper," I finish up. "As you look at the graves, he's on the left side of Miss Sarah. We didn't know what to put on his marker."

The fire makes the only sound in the camp for a long time. There's nothing for anybody to say, I guess. I can tell she wants to ask me about Sarah, but to her credit she doesn't.

We don't do a whole lot more talking before we turn in, but we do find out that Daga is her brother-in-law and he brought her up to see where her brother rests. He beds down across the fire from me and James, pistol close to hand. A pretty careful man, Mr. Daga.

Clouds have blown in during the night, and morning comes gray and dull. James cooks thick slices of ham, the last of our eggs, potatoes, and coffee. Daga eats like he's trying to fill up both legs, and I got to admit I do too.

James winces a little when he mounts up, but I don't fault him any, because he can't be used to riding as much as we are. He doesn't complain, though, and day two goes pretty much the same as day one. Daga and Miss Luis are going to turn south in the morning, and I can tell that James is troubled some by the idea of watching her ride away from him. They sit up late by the dying embers, and Daga and I finally turn in without them. I drift off to sleep to the quiet sound of their subdued voices.

Miss Luis walks off a piece by herself in the morning, and James starts cooking. Miss Luis is not yet back by the time the food is ready, and Daga gets more and more nervous and finally goes looking for her. When he returns his face is tight and angry, and I wouldn't want him to look at me in that way. He's fixing to kill someone for sure. He throws his saddle up, saddles her horse, and rides off without a word to either of us. James and I sit there and watch him go.

"What's going on?" James asks.

"Don't know."

"Well, go find out!" he says, and he's not very nice about it, either. I don't much like people telling me what to do in that tone of voice, but he's my friend and I know he's upset about Miss Luis, so I don't pay him no mind.

"Okay," I say as I get up. "But you might as well come along." We break camp, and it hurts me to see him dump a full pot of coffee on the fire. I sure would have liked to have some before we leave.

The tracks are plain as day. Miss Luis was walking back to camp when two men grabbed her. She struggled some, but they lifted her up and took her back to the east. I explain it to James, and this civilized man from Boston gets the same killing expression that Daga had. I guess being civilized just means that the man is covered up some by manners, not that his teeth have been pulled.

It isn't much farther on before we run across Daga ranging back and forth, trying to pick up their trail. I can follow them across the rocks some, and pretty soon we find a piece of folded paper stuck under a rock. My four rifle bullets are standing on the paper. I give the paper to James and he opens it up.

"They say they want what we're after," he tells me. "They will not harm her, and we can have her back as soon as they have the gold." He looks up at me and I can see the worry in his eyes. "Do you suppose they are telling the truth?" he wants to know.

"It's not likely that a man will hurt a woman out here," I say. "There are not too many of them and it would turn every man's hand against them." He seems eased by my explanation.

"You know where gold is?" Daga asks. I guess he can talk English after all.

"I got the map those men were all willing to die for," I answer.

"What are you going to do, Señor Walker?"

It doesn't seem right, somehow, that it's always the innocent who got to do the most suffering. Poor Sarah never hurt nobody, but they killed her, anyhow. Now it's Miss Luis. This map has brought nothing but trouble to the innocent and nothing but grief to the people who have held it.

"We'll take them to the cache," I say, cold

and hard. "And if they hurt Miss Luis, we'll kill them!"

"You will just give them the gold?" James sounds surprised.

"We don't know that there really is any gold there. If there is, it has brought nobody anything good," I tell him. "These skunks sure deserve some of that."

He seems satisfied, but Daga looks at me hard.

"Write them an answer," I tell James. "Say we'll give them the gold, but we'll want to see that Miss Luis hasn't been hurt tomorrow morning before we show them where it is. If she has been hurt in any way, we'll destroy the map and kill them all. For sure!"

James writes for a long time and then puts the paper down on the rock, holding it in place with the rifle shells. I should have put those shells into those four fellows, I guess. This is what I get for being so soft.

We mount and ride for the cache of gold. I keep moving fast, on account of I don't want those behind us to be able to stop. If we give them too much free time, they might start noticing how pretty Miss Luis is, and that's something I don't wish to happen. Besides, if I get them good and worn out, they might make some kind of mistake when they hadn't ought to.

I haven't told James, but these desperate men have got no choice but to kill us all once they have the gold. If there is any gold. They don't want us hunting them, and also they don't want to leave anybody around who can point them out to the law at some later time. I think Daga knows all that without being told.

And so we ride, wearing out ourselves and our horses, riding until nightfall and it's too dark to be safe. I build a big fire, and we cook up the last of the ham and some coffee. James is plumb wore out and can hardly keep his eyes open while he eats. Then he rolls into his bedroll without even saying good night.

"He's doing real good for his first time out," I say to Daga.

"He does not complain, and that's a good sign." He finishes his coffee and sighs. "We are going after them now?" he finally says.

"Seems like a good idea to me," I say back. I knew he was smart.

We make up our bedrolls so they look like we're in them, then walk out of the firelight and into the dark. Daga is as quiet as I am while we quiet-step through the night. Maybe he spent some time with the Indians too.

The sky is all full of stars, and they twinkle hard and bright over the land. They watch everything that happens and don't care anything about any of it. Tonight there will likely be hard trouble, but the sky is no different from any other night. Funny how much better a man can see the sky out here than he can in Boston. Prob'ly something to do with all the lights around in the big city. Thinking of Boston makes me wonder what Nancy is doing right this minute while I'm out here hunting men. Prob'ly sleeping by now, I suppose.

Their camp is farther away than I thought, and it takes us most of two hours to find it. I believe I could have picked a better spot to camp were I them. Too many big rocks around for a man to hide behind. Daga and I settle down behind one of them and study the situation.

They are bedded down in a circle of big rocks and, counting the horses, there must be just the four of them plus Miss Luis. One of them is on guard, sitting on top of one of the rocks.

First thing is to put the sentry out of action. The fact that he's up high means we can't sneak up on him, so I slide my knife out and get ready to throw it into him. It's kind of risky, on account of he may holler when he's stuck, but I can't see any other way to get him out of the action.

Daga touches my arm and shakes his head, telling me to wait. He must have some other idea, which is fine with me, on account of I really don't want to kill anybody unless I have to. He picks up a rock the size of a man's fist and hefts it. He smiles at me, and then I hear his soft steps off into the night. I settle down to watch and wait. Pretty soon I see his arm come up from behind a rock by the sentry, and he rears back and lets fly. It's a good throw, especially in the dark from that distance. The rock hits the guard just behind the ear with a satisfying thud, and he slumps forward just like he fell asleep.

The other three are rolled up like Christmas presents, and Daga and I soft-step in among them before they even know there's anything wrong. Daga puts a meaty hand over Miss Luis's mouth and she comes stiff all at once as she wakes up. He picks her up, bedroll and all, and I back out of the camp behind them, making sure that none of them wake up and spoil the party. It all seems too easy, and it is, because one of them opens his eyes, takes in the situation, and starts to move quick.

Boom! the sound of my .45 jerks them all awake, and the one who was moving stops real sudden as the slug smacks into the dirt right next to him.

"That could have been in your head," I explain to him, but I think he prob'ly knew that already. "We got the girl back and we'll be leaving now," I go on. I am not talking too loud, but they seem to be hangin' on every word. "This is the second time I could have killed you but I didn't. There's not goin' to be any third time." They don't say anything, just lie there and take it all in. "We'll be taking your horses," I add. No sense in leaving them a means to follow us too easily. "You'd be real smart if you just rolled over and went back to sleep like your buddy who was standing guard." For a minute, I believe they're going to be real smart, but the one farthest away from the fire moves real quick and comes up with a gun. I can hear Daga cutting the horses loose, so he doesn't figure to be any help in this at all.

"Walker! Look out!" Miss Luis calls from off in the dark, and I commence to shooting. They're all grabbing for guns and rolling around on the ground, trying to make it hard to hit them. I know my first shot hits the far man with the gun, on account of I hear the smack of the lead striking his bedroll, and, besides, he grunts real hard.

A gun flashes from the ground, and I hear the slug whine past my right ear. The man is shooting too fast and fails to take that extra second to aim, and he pays the price as my lead thuds into him lying there. The gun flies from his hand, and I turn my attention to the other man, and for a second we're looking at each other eyeball to eyeball, only his gun is already pointing at me and mine is just starting to swing on him and I know I'm about to be shot. But he slams back against the ground, and a second later the sound of a distant rifle tells me what done him in.

Daga comes charging up, pistol in hand, and I can tell he's just as surprised as I am at the rifle shot. It can only be one other person, and it is. James comes hotfooting it into camp, rifle looking small in his big hands.

"Glad to see you," I say to him.

"I believe you," he comes back.

Miss Luis runs to him and gives him a big hug. Daga and I, the two what rescued her in the first place, just sort of look at each other.

We didn't get any hug, and, in fact, I haven't even got a polite thank you.

It is a pretty long hug, and they're sort of taken aback by the fact that they're hanging on to each other. Nor does either of them seem particular anxious to let go. Daga is going to have some explaining to do to her folks when he gets her back, on account of the Mexicans are pretty careful about their women. He grumbles something in Spanish, and Miss Luis drops her arms and steps back real sudden.

James's blood is running hot, but he's a smart man, and he turns away and walks slowly over to the fire while all three of us watch. He bends down and pours a cup of coffee out of the pot like nothing unusual happened and there are not three bodies lying there. I got to say, it's one of the coolest moves I have ever seen a man make after a shooting incident, and he has our attention as he sips at the hot stuff, makes a sour face, and tosses it hissing into the fire.

Miss Luis never takes her eyes off him, and it's plain she thinks he is some very special kind of man. I do too, and even Daga has to admire his calm. James looks me in the eye, but I can read nothing of him in there. I think maybe this romantic situation is plumb out of control, and I fear for the way it's all going to come out in the end.

"What about the guard?" Daga asks.

"Leave him," I say. "We'll leave a horse for him, and if he's at all smart, he'll bury his friends and ride away."

We take their food since they're not going to need it anymore, and all the other horses too, and head back to camp. Lightning far off in the west announces that we're soon to be wet by one of the infrequent thunderstorms we have out here. I'm already feeling low because we had to kill those men, so I don't mind the idea of getting a little wet. Sort of like a punishment from above.

It holds off and we get back to camp, although the flashes of lightning and the thunder are getting closer all the time. James builds up the fire and makes coffee in silence. He's madder than a wet hen because we left and didn't tell him where we were going. I guess he has a point, especially since that makes two times he has saved my life. He hands me a cup in silence.

"I underestimated you," I say. "Won't happen again."

He looks me in the eye. "Good," he says back.

We all go to work on the coffee, and I think a bit on our situation. "Like it or not," I finally say, "you two are involved in this as deep as we are. There's likely more people after us and they believe we're all in it together. Even if you split off and head south, they'd likely believe it was a trick and send some men after you. Only way to get clear of them is to give them what they want."

"Unless we can lose them in the rain," Daga says.

I think he'd like to keep the gold if he can, and I'm not really surprised that he seems to think part of that gold should be his. Men never seem to think straight when gold is involved, so I don't really blame him any.

"That doesn't seem likely," I say. "They must have some pretty fair trackers among them."

Daga nods in agreement, but I can tell he doesn't like the idea of giving up wealth to bandits.

"We will lead them right to it," I go on. "Only thing, we have to think how to keep them from killing us when we do."

"Surely they will have no need to kill us once they have the gold," Miss Luis says.

"Ma'am," I explain, "while it's true there's very little law out here, these men know that

Daga and me would likely come after them. Only way to prevent that is for them to kill us."

She looks to Daga. He nods in agreement. "This is indeed a brutal land," she says.

"It is that," I agree.

"So what are we going to do?" James asks.

"We're only a few hours away from the spot," I say. "I figure to take our rifles, ride to the spot, and hide them where we can maybe get to them during the proceedings. Might be we can figure a way to drop one of us off and have him cover the rest of us." I heave to my feet. "Finish the coffee and head out due west. I'll meet you sometime after sunrise."

Daga nods, so I know it'll be done.

It's late, and I'd like to sit and have coffee with them, but it's a job only I can do, so I take their rifles, mount up, and ride out. I can feel them watching me, but nobody says anything.

They are eating breakfast in a good spot, back to a hill, when I ride into them once more. James is relieved to see me. Just as I hunker down by the fire, the rain finally comes, slowly at first, then faster and faster. The wind picks up, and it becomes plenty uncomfortable with the water blowing against us and the wind chilling us down. We get our slickers on as quick as we can, then try to finish up with the eating.

I watch water make little splashes in my coffee, and I can feel it running off the back of my hat and down my slicker.

"Hope those men behind are as uncomfortable as I am," James says.

"Prob'ly are," I say. "There are ten of them maybe half a mile behind us. Watching us right now, I expect."

James starts to turn to look, but thinks better of it right away. I knew he was going to be a good man in the wilderness. Daga knew better right away, and he doesn't move at all. I'm sure he knows there's a single man hiding behind that rock and listening to what we're saying. I'm sure James and Miss Luis do not know.

"What are we going to do now?" Miss Luis wants to know.

"I believe it would be best to ride to where the gold is supposed to be," I say. "I think if we lead them to it and then ride off, they might be too busy to come after us."

"Are you going to let them have the gold?" James asks one last time.

"I wouldn't know how to act as a rich man," I reply. "And I for sure wouldn't know how to act as a dead one." I'm talking pretty loud so that the skunk hiding over there can hear me plain.

"Good point," James mutters.

If it had rained earlier, the bandits might have lost our trail for good, but now that they have us in sight, all the rain does is make us chilly and miserable. Them too, I hope.

The horses plod on through the rocks and mud, and in two hours we are there. I have hidden the rifles behind three different rocks around the perimeter, and I whisper to the others where they are. James drops behind like he's looking for a spot to do something private, and Daga, Miss Luis, and I ride on in.

The two small hills are right where the map said, and after a few minutes of lookin' around in the mud, I find the skull of a mule. I toss it aside and turn over a couple of shovels of mud when the bandits come riding down on us from all around. There's no chance for escape, and Daga and I get back together with Miss Luis in the middle. We each have our pistol in our hand.

"Don't shoot until I say so," I say.

Even though it's ten against two, they're not real eager to start any shooting, on account of they don't know for sure if I led them to the right place. Besides, they know that some of them will be dead before we are, and I've never yet seen a man eager to die. They ride down, making a tighter circle around us, and for a while we all sort of just look at one another, waiting to see what happens next.

"Drop your guns," one of them says.

I look at him hard. It is Craighton Richards, and he's a known badman, but not a cold killer.

"No," I say right back. I can see them thinking it over and liking it none.

"If you're counting on the tenderfoot for help, you can forget it," he says. "Two of my men are watching him."

"Don't need his help to kill you and some of them too," I say back.

He thinks on that, and I can see it doesn't set real good with him. He knows that if he starts anything, he'll be the first one I shoot, and he's not real anxious to have that happen.

"Then step aside," he says. "If the gold is there, you can go on about your business and no harm done."

"Fair enough," I say, and we move by our horses. Three of them stay with us, careful to keep their hands away from their guns. The rest dismount and start digging. I can tell that Daga is just as curious as the badmen to find out what's buried under that skull.

They haven't dug into the mud too long when one of them shouts and everybody gets excited. He tosses out a deerskin bag, then another. Craighton opens one of them and shows a handful of gold nuggets to the rest. While a cheer goes up from the men, we try to back away in the confusion, but Craighton nods a signal and the war is on.

Daga turns out to be a fair hand with a gun, and his first shot is only a second behind mine, but we both picked the same guard. The two slugs send him flying backward into one of his friends, and Daga and I each put a round into the one still standing.

The big group over by the gold have got their guns into action, and our spot seems like an unhealthy place to be as bullets buzz around like bees. Daga takes Miss Luis by the hand and yanks her behind a horse as they start running. Bullets smack into the horse and it goes down screaming into the mud.

Daga and Miss Luis are heading for the nearest rocks that have a rifle hid, and I am thumbing off shots into the group while they run. One man goes down hard, and another grabs at his arm and drops his gun before I'm empty. Seems pretty foolish to be standing there with an empty gun, so I take off too, trying to keep the horses between me and them as long as possible.

Daga has picked the closest rifle, and I can't blame him any, although that means I got to run a little farther before I get any artillery. I zigzag across the ground, seeing puddles splash up in my face as bullets smack into them, and it's only a matter of time before one of them gets lucky. I feel a bullet tug at my shirt and hear the banging of their guns and the screaming of injured horses. I am almost to the rocks when I hear Daga open up with the rifle, working the lever like a pump handle on a winter day.

BOOM! BOOM! BOOM! The pistol fire thins out some as they face-down into the mud to get away from his fire. I dive headfirst over the big rock, hearing two slugs scream off it just as I get to safety. I'm panting like crazy and there's no doubt whatever that my heart is working at its best rate. A Winchester has never felt better to my hands as I pick up the rifle and peer around the side of the rock.

All three of our horses are down, one motion-less and the other two kicking and screaming in the mud. Two measured shots from some-body down there ends the poor animals' suffering, and silence settles over the area. I am amazed. Seems like none of us has been hit hard, and I can count three of them down for good and one hurt. The rest have taken cover just like us, and the two bags of gold are just lying there in the mud with no living soul around them.

The rain keeps beating down, and it seems like things are at a draw for the time being. I wonder what happened to James and the two men who were watching him.

Chapter Nine

"Hey, Walker!" I hear Craighton call from somewhere in the rain. "You dead yet?"

"Not even a little bit!" I yell back.

There's a pause while he digests that. I listen to the rain splat on the brim of my soaked hat while I shuck the empty hulls and stuff shells into my empty gun and slip it back into the holster.

"You don't have no chance at all!" he finally yells. "There are ten of us and only three of you."

"The way I count, there are only six of you left," I call back. "You started out with fourteen yesterday and haven't got any of us yet. Maybe it's you guys who ought to ride out."

A rifle cracks from over by where we dropped James off. Then it fires again and again. The sound is flattened by the rain. I see a man run down from the rocks and flatten out on the ground below. In the rain I can't tell if it's James or not.

"I say! Walker!" James calls from over by the rock. "There are only five of them left now!"

A long silence from down below.

"I got more coming, Walker!" Craighton yells. "They'll be here by tomorrow morning."

I don't know whether to believe him or not. Don't see that I can take a chance on him lying, though.

"How many bags of gold you figure are down there?" I yell at him. It's my plan to get him thinking about the gold, so they'll dig for a while after we make our escape.

"Not enough for you to get any!" he yells back.

I think he may be down by a clump of rocks over to the left of the bags, but he's well hidden and I don't think I can do him any damage from here.

A slug slams off the rock in front of me, followed instantly by the sound of the rifle from down below. It's a good, solid rock and I'm growing rather fond of it.

"How'd you like that, Walker?" It is a different voice from down below. Sounds like it's more to the right than where Craighton is hidden. I line up my sights on the next pile of rocks over. Maybe the rifleman is dumb enough to stick his fat head up for a look. I don't answer his taunt.

Suddenly a hat spears into sight. Since it's hanging funny, like it's on a stick, I don't do any shooting. The hat sinks from view. In a half minute, what could be the top of a head slowly raises over the rock. When my rifle goes off, it's almost a surprise, the sign of a good shot. The head drops from sight and I can hear someone cursing hard and long over the sound of the rain.

It's plain they'll come after us once they have the gold, and that only leaves one thing I can do. I line up the sights on the farthest horse, not liking what I'm going to do at all, and I squeeze the trigger. I work the lever, aim at another, and fire again and once more before the cursing men from below direct so much fire against my rock that I'm forced to take cover. Slug after slug whines off the rock, and one or two buzz angrily over and around as they try to stop me. I hear the bark of Daga's rifle, and then James chips in from the other side. In a minute it's all over and it seems like there are dead horses everywhere down there.

The rain is letting up at last, diminishing to small drops that peck lightly on my hat and slicker.

"Walker!" It is Craighton, and his voice is tight with fury. "You're a dead man."

I don't blame him for being angry. Watching perfectly good horses slaughtered would peeve me some too. "Craighton!" I call back. "We're leaving here in the dark of night. You can have the gold and welcome to it, but once you have it, don't come after us if you want to live long enough to spend it."

"I'll have more men with horses by tomorrow," he answers. "You're not in any position to threaten me."

"Take the gold and go. Anything else will bring you grief."

Another shot smacks off the rock in answer. My rock is at the crest of one of the two hills, so James doesn't have any trouble getting behind me, and when I look back, he's standing down there looking up at me. I belly-slide back until it's safe to stand and go down to meet him. There's blood on the front of his shirt.

"Howdy," I say. "You okay?"

"One of them stuck me with a knife before I was able to dispatch him properly," he tells me.

"Let me take a look," I say, only I never get a chance, because Miss Luis squeals and comes running up. She makes him sit down and opens his shirt and just sort of takes over like she owns him, and I guess, in a way, she does. Daga comes walking up. His face is hard to read as he watches her tend to the wound. It doesn't look like James has been hurt too bad. The blade opened a long cut, but it's only skin deep.

"Once she has him fixed, you people start walking back toward the station," I say. "I'll stay here for about an hour after you leave and make them think twice about following along."

Daga nods. "We will wait where we had breakfast this morning," he says.

"I'll find you. But if I'm not there in an hour. . . ."

He nods. "We will go on and trust in you to find us," he says.

Miss Luis has come up with a needle and thread from somewhere. Danged if women aren't surprising me all the time. Soon she's busy sewing the wound closed and James is busy turning white. She seems to know what she's doing pretty good. The last stitch goes in, and she tears a strip off the bottom of his shirt and binds the wound with it. When he puts the shirt back on, it doesn't reach all the way to his pants and he looks down at himself. I can tell he's not used to being poorly dressed, and it doesn't sit with him too well. 'Course, he isn't used to being knifed, and that prob'ly doesn't sit too well with him, either.

"You find something funny in all this?" he asks me.

I didn't know I'd been smiling even a little. "I do not for sure," I say back. "I'm just glad you were not hurt worse."

"It appeared to me as though you were amused at my suffering." He's as grouchy as an old bear, and even Miss Luis is glaring at me.

"I was just wondering what was bigger, the knife that cut you or the needle she sewed you with," I say back.

Sometimes my mouth seems to have a mind of its own. James turns red, and all of a sudden Miss Luis is standing in front of me, hands fisted on hips and real close. For an instant she reminds me of Nancy. She waves the needle under my chin, and I got to admit that in her hands, it does appear about the size of a knife.

"Mr. Walker," she says through gritted teeth, "it appears you have something open that could use a little sewing too."

I'm amazed, and feel my eyes open wide in surprise. I never figured her for this kind of spunk, and I back a step away from her. She is like a she-bear protecting her cub. James's eyes are open wide too, and Daga is grinning wide enough to split his face clean in half. I got no idea what to do next, so I heft my rifle and head back up to the rock.

"You'd better get back up there where you are safe," James says behind me, and then he laughs. "First time I ever saw you run away from anything, Walker." As he laughs again, I feel a grin split my face, and shake my head in wonderment. That Miss Luis is certainly a woman to cross the river with. James could do a lot worse, I'm thinking.

They have been gone about a half hour before the men down below begin to get restless.

"Hey, Walker!" Craighton yells. "You dead yet?"

I don't answer, and another fifteen minutes goes by.

"Hey, Walker! Are you still there?"

I don't say anything. Maybe they're going to do something stupid. In another minute, sure enough, a hat on a stick comes up from behind some rocks. They must think I am stupid or something.

"I think they're gone," one of them says.

"Why don't you stick your dumb head up and find out for sure?" another comes back.

"Just 'cause I think they're gone don't make me dumb," says the first one.

"It does if you stick your head up and they're still there," his friend answers.

Their palaver makes me want to smile. They call me some more, but I don't say anything, of course. Pretty soon a head comes up from behind the rocks. Up and down, real quick. I thumb back the hammer and sight on the spot. Shooting downhill means you got to aim a little low, so I line up the sights on the edge of the rock and wait. Up and down goes the head again, but I still got a little time, so I wait patiently. Might be I can lower the odds some.

"I believe they *are* gone," says the one.

"Don't do nothing stupid," calls his friend.

"I ain't gonna do nothing stupid. They *are* gone. I stuck my head up there twice."

"They prob'ly ain't shooting on account of the target ain't worth much," from the other one.

"I don't know why you're always saying such bad things about me," the first one whines. "I ain't stupid, you know."

"I seen you shoot your own toe off once because you was standing on a snake," the first one comes back. "That don't seem real bright to me."

"I only done it once," from the first one.

I feel myself grin.

"You sure learn fast," from his friend.

"I am going to stand up," from the first.

"Stay down, Webb," his friend says.

"They're gone, I tell you," Webb says.

"No, they ain't."

"Here goes." And suddenly Webb stands tall behind the rock.

Somehow, I don't have it in me to kill him, although he'd likely do me in if he got the chance. I move the sight until it is just below his right shoulder and squeeze easy on the trigger.

BOOM! And he flips backward as the slug smashes home. It's real quiet down there for maybe five minutes.

"Hey, Ritchy," Webb calls. He don't sound a bit dead.

"What?"

"I think they're still up there," Webb answers. Ritchy starts cursing, and I can still hear him cussing out his friend as I slide down and start walking after the others. Makes me smile for quite a while.

If I figure it right, they aren't about to do anything else real stupid until dark. That gives us a six-hour start at least. Then, if they wait until morning so they can dig up the treasure, we got another ten hours. 'Course, if they really do have help coming with horses, sixteen hours may not be near enough. But we'll have to deal with that if it happens.

The rain has stopped and it's easy to follow my friends. Now there is a word I don't use too often.

They have a fire going, and Daga is cooking rabbits on a spit. James is lying with his head in Miss Luis's lap, hand over his closed eyes. Daga looks at them now and then, disgusted.

"I do not think he's hurt all that bad," Daga says to me when I walk up.

I smile. "Nobody ever said he was stupid," I say back. Daga just grunts. I guess he has realized he can do nothing about the two of them. He slides off a piece of rabbit and hands it to me.

"You get any more of them?" he asks.

"Wounded one. I figure we got maybe sixteen hours on them," I say as I chew.

James gets up and takes some rabbit for Miss Luis and himself. He says, "Sixteen hours should be sufficient to permit us to return to the relative civilization of the station, I believe."

"Time we get done eating here. We will have only fifteen hours," I point out. "If they really do get horses, our lead will be cut, and they'll be on us four or five hours after that, shortly after noontime tomorrow."

"What do you want us to do, Mr. Walker?" Miss Luis asks.

"Well, ma'am," I say, "I think we should walk a piece tonight yet. We are maybe six hours' hard walk from those hills over there, and once in there, we can take care of ourselves if need be."

"You are familiar with those hills?" she asks.

"That I am. I used to hunt there quite regular."

"Mr. Walker," she says real stiffly and formally after a minute, "I wish to apologize for my behavior back there."

"That's okay. I'm just glad I didn't have to shoot you."

She starts a little at that, not quite sure how to take it until James barks a laugh. Right away she thinks I'm making fun of her.

"Mr. Walker," she says all huffy, "I can see why you must resort to violence so often."

Now I am took back and can think of nothing to say. We eat in stiff silence. James keeps looking over at me and smirking. That small woman has sure made a mighty change in that big, quiet man. Once, only a week ago, he was content to wait on other folks and make their lives easier at the expense of his own. Now he's a man full grown, standing on his own hind legs and going after what *he* wants. Must be something in this Western air, I'm thinking.

Chapter Ten

It has been dark almost two hours and the moon is peeking out from behind racing clouds when we get into the hills far enough for me to feel safer. I know a good spot we can make by noontime where we can wait and be safe if they come. If they don't, it won't hurt any to wait a couple of hours.

James hasn't said anything at all for a couple of hours, but I can see he's getting worn out and needs to rest. I think back on when I first saw him in his undertaker suit and am amazed at what a real man those fancy duds hid. He settles against a rock with a big sigh and Miss Luis sits right next to him.

"I will take the first watch," Daga says, and I am glad, because I'm plumb worn out myself. Also, I'm not quite all healed up yet

167

from the trouble at Doc's house. Ordinarily, I could walk all day and all night without getting tired. Maybe I'm just getting old. I lay back on the hard dirt and let my eyes slide closed, trusting in Daga to keep us all safe for a while.

I am back in Sarah's bedroom, lying in the bed with her, but she keeps changing from Sarah to Nancy and back again. They are both dying and I feel all the hurt from before, only worse. I don't want them to die. "Don't die," I say to them. "Don't die, Nancy." It's a confusing dream, and the hours of sleep soak away into the hard dirt.

"Wake up." And a hand shakes my shoulder gently. It's a woman's hand. Nancy?

"Don't die," I say. "Please don't die."

"Wake up, Señor Walker."

I open my eyes. The sky is red with the morning light and Miss Luis is pushing on my shoulder. She's looking at me strangely, and all of a sudden I feel tears on my cheeks. Shame rushes through me and I jump to my feet and turn away. Heat rushes to my face and I wipe my face with my sleeve. When I turn back, Miss Luis has gone over to James and sat down once more.

I cannot accept that I have slept the entire

night through while these others, including a young woman, have watched over me. It doesn't seem right, somehow. I do have to admit I feel a lot better, though.

"All right, folks," I say, "time to get walking."

They get to their feet, and I lead off into the hills. They follow along uncomplaining, trusting in me.

It's about an hour before noon when I lead them into a little valley. The entrance is maybe a man on a horse wide, and it opens into a small grassy meadow that's less than an easy rifle shot across. We walk through the grass and turn left when the meadow does. Suddenly, we are up against a rock wall maybe twenty feet high, and I climb up to the top.

"Here is where we'll wait for them," I say. "Daga and James will take Miss Luis and set up halfway back on that side, and I'll go along this side about the same distance."

"I am quite capable of shooting a rifle or a pistol, Mr. Walker," Miss Luis says. "I would like to help."

"I believe you, ma'am," I say back, "only it doesn't seem right for a woman to be taking chances like that. These are bad men and. . . ."

Her hands fist up and park on her hips. I

have seen that stance before, and didn't like it much, either.

"Mr. Walker!" she says hard.

"Okay, okay, ma'am. No need to get all ruffled up. I never did like telling people what to do, anyhow. I'm going to get behind some rocks on this side. You folks just do what you think is best." I proceed to follow words with action, and walk back about halfway and plant myself in a decent spot behind some rocks. My rifle will cover the entire valley from here.

Daga walks up the other side and parks close to the entrance. James parks farther in. Anybody who comes into this valley is going to be under our guns for sure. I am kind of surprised when Miss Luis comes up and sits down with me.

"I did not mean to offend you," she says.

"No offense taken, ma'am."

"Good. Now if you will allow me the use of your pistol, I will try to be of some value."

I take off the belt and hand it to her. "There are six in it and twelve left in the belt," I say. "Make them count."

We sit in silence for a while. "Will they come?" she asks.

"I wouldn't be surprised. We'll know for sure in a couple of hours."

She nods and once again silence falls. I can hear an eagle calling way off in the distance.

"Did you really shoot her?" she asks.

I look at her, and she looks me direct in the eye, waiting for my answer. It's none of her business, really, but I find I want to tell her, maybe on account of she's a woman and can tell me if I did right.

And so I tell her. I tell her of the strangeness of going into the kitchen for the first time. I tell her of the awful sickness when I found out Sarah had been shot. I tell about the lying in bed together and the wolves howling outside, and I tell her about how I can tell if my gun is loaded or empty just from the weight as it hangs on my hip. I tell her about how I didn't notice it was missing when I went outside even though I really had to know it was missing. And I tell her about how Sarah took the same gun she was holding right now and put it to her heart and shot herself. I tell her about the miserable sadness when I went back inside and how we lay together through the long, awful night. And then I look over at Miss Luis and she is crying but not making any sound. Tears are leaking out and running down her smooth cheeks.

"I'm sorry," I say. "I truly wouldn't have made you cry for anything at all. I guess I shouldn't have told you after all."

"No," she says as she wipes her cheeks, "I am glad you told me."

"I'm not sure I knew what she was going to do," I say. "But I had to know inside, I guess. Do you think I did the right thing?" I ask.

It's the question I have wanted to ask someone ever since it happened, only there hasn't been anyone I could ask who would maybe understand. I almost hold my breath waiting for the answer. She thinks a long time on the question.

"I would hope someone would care enough about me to do the same thing," she says softly.

I let out a big sigh. It is like someone has taken poison out of me, and all of a sudden I know I didn't do an evil thing.

"I'm glad to hear you say that, ma'am," I reply.

Once again silence falls. This time, though, it is not a hard quiet, but rather a softer, more easy one.

The first rider pokes his nose into the valley about an hour later. It is the fellow I shot in the shoulder yesterday. He has a white bandage and is wearing the arm in a sling as he guides his horse into the valley, following our tracks. He must be the best tracker they have. I knew I should have shot him better yesterday. I must be getting soft, but I am so tired of seeing dead men.

He reins in and looks over the valley, and I can tell he doesn't like the setup at all, because he can easily see that our tracks go in but don't come out. From where he is, he can't tell the valley is a trap. I almost feel sorry for him. He studies on it for quite a while, then turns and motions to his buddies who have been waiting outside.

There are six of them, riding horses that I haven't seen before. Craighton is among them. There are prob'ly more of them afoot somewhere behind.

Craighton looks around, not liking the setup any more than the first man. The first man, Webb, kicks his horse into motion and they ride in deeper until they can all of a sudden see that they have ridden into a trap. They stop and look up at the walls.

"I warned you, Craighton!" I holler down. "If you want to live, get off those horses and walk on out of here!"

Craighton looks up at where I am, and I can see the anger. He is not any kind of a fool, though, and he knows he's under our guns good and proper.

"There are more men coming!" he yells back.

"You told me that yesterday too, and look where it got you," I say right back. "I'm tired of killing you people and have no want to kill more of you, but I will if I have to."

They are confused, and they mill around, tryin' to decide what to do. Craighton boots his horse into a slow walk and heads for the opening. I put a rifle shot ahead of him and he stops.

"I said leave the horses!" I yell. "You can keep the gold and I'll not come after you, but if you try to get the horses out of here, I'll kill you for sure."

He thinks on that, and then he turns his horse and looks up at where I am. Most likely, he can see my rifle pointing at him.

"Do you give your word you won't hunt us down?" he asks.

"I give you my word. I don't much care about the gold, but I care about these people with me, and we could sure use those horses. It's the best deal you're likely to get," I add.

He swings down and takes the saddlebags

off the horse. Ground-tied, the horse stands easy. The others swing down too. Maybe this is going to turn out for the best after all.

"Leave the saddlebags," I say. "Maybe living off the land for a few days will be good for you."

I can see they don't like the idea, but they don't really have much choice. They walk toward the opening, leaving the horses behind. Webb is already pasty white, weak from his wound.

"Webb," I call, and he stops like he's been shot. "You can ride in with us, if you've a mind to."

He nods and sits down on a handy rock. "Thank you kindly," he says.

"Least I can do, since I'm the one who shot you," I answer while the rest of them walk to the opening. "Hey, Craighton!" I call.

"Yeah?" He stops.

"How many bags did you find?"

"Three," he said. "Not hardly enough to go around."

I believe him. "Maybe you should try honest work," I say back.

He looks up at where I am and grins. "I ain't that desperate yet," he says, and walks out of the valley.

We walk down to the horses while Webb watches us come, and Daga mounts up and rides out to make sure they're not going to be any more trouble. I'm glad we didn't have to kill anyone else.

"You could have killed me just as easy, couldn't you?" Webb asks.

"I found it hard to kill a man who shot off his own toe," I explain.

He looks disgusted. "Man makes one mistake and his friends never let him forget it," he says.

I have to help him mount on account of his bad arm. I am glad I didn't kill him.

We retrace our route back toward the station in silence. The ground is mostly dry by suppertime. We go through their saddlebags for supplies, and James works wonders with some stew that we sit around and eat from our metal plates.

"Are you disappointed, Mr. Walker?" Miss Luis wants to know. She and James are sitting side by side.

"Just glad to be alive."

"But all that gold," she says right back.

"Weren't so much," I say. "Prob'ly just enough that those men may start shooting each other for it, but not nearly enough to live rich for the rest of their lives. If I know those kind of men, it will all be spent before the end of the year."

"You are probably right, Walker," James says. "No good comes of ill-gotten money like that."

"James," I say with a smile, "money has got no conscience and neither do those men who took it. But it's not going to last them long, and it's going to seem like it wasn't worth the trouble after they've been on the lam for a year or so." I turn to Miss Luis. "You going back to the station with us, ma'am?"

"Yes," she says, and I can see the relief on James's face. "Now that I know which is his grave, I would like to put a decent marker over my brother, one with his name, one that will last."

"I think that is a mighty fine idea," I say. "I wish we could put one over the dude and the kid who also died, but I suppose we'll never know who they were. Somewhere their families must be wondering and worrying."

Two days later we top the rise overlooking the station. It looks the same from up here, and it seems so long ago that I considered that place home. But I got no home at all now. James sidles up to me. "I'm going to marry her," he says.

I look him over some. "Does she know that yet?" I ask.

"Yes. I asked her last night."

"And she said yes?"

"No," he admits. "She said it was her custom to have her parents' permission before she could marry."

"So you'll be going to Mexico?" I ask. I already know the answer. There is not much in this world more powerful than the want of a woman.

"Yes," he says, "I'll be going back with them."

"Daga know about this?"

"Yes. He wasn't very impressed, I'm afraid."

I shake his hand. "He will be by the time you get there. You're a good man, James Dagget."

"So are you, John Walker."

We ride along to the station. James has set himself a tough row to hoe, because Mexican families aren't too keen to take foreigners for a son-in-law. 'Course, he is strong and a fighter, so in the end I don't think they'll be able to turn him out. Daga will prob'ly vouch for James by the time they get down there.

And just like that, a man's life is laid out for him. He will travel to Mexico, win over the family of his woman, and marry her. They will live and love together without ever being lonely again. Prob'ly have children and raise them up together. If they are real lucky, they will grow old together, and the only time they'll ever be alone is the short time between when one of them passes on and the other one does.

It seems that every time I make a friend, something happens and then I am by myself again. I guess it's good that I've spent so much time alone, on account of it doesn't scare me like it might someone else.

I've come close, though. Sarah and I could have gone through life together 'cept for that stray shot. The only other women I know are Miss Emily, who I wouldn't have, and Miss Nancy, who wouldn't have me on account of I'm a barbarian. I would have *her,* though.

I am surprised at my feelings about her. When we were together, it seemed like we were fighting all the time, and yet I miss her now. She was spunky and cute, and I remember her arm under my head when she was healing me. She was the kind who would stand by a man no matter what, and carry her share of the load too. I sure miss her, and I wish she was here. Seems like my life is all laid out for me too, only it's not nearly as nice as what James has ahead of him.

The old man at the station treats me like he's scared of me, and it makes me sorry for what I did the last time I was here. He feeds us a noon meal that's hardly fit to eat, and then he goes out to get the horses ready for the morning stage, which is running late as usual. As I watch him harness the horses, I remember when I used to do that. Then I walk around the back to the graves.

The grass is growing on them, and a man would be hard put to say how old they were if he didn't already know. I take off my hat and look down on Sarah's final resting place. I hope she has finally got the peace she so deserved. I wish I could tell her how I fooled all them fellows. She would prob'ly get a kick out of it. Bet Nancy would too.

It cost me only a little sleep to find that skull, dig up three bags, and bury them off to the other side. It made me smile when I put the skull on them, knowing the rain would cover my tracks and they would think the three bags were the whole treasure. Must be twenty more under there yet, and I'm the only one who knows where they are. I had in my mind to get them later, buy a nice ranch

omewhere, and spend the rest of my life with
Miss Nancy if she would have me.

Funny how my insides get all messed up
about Sarah and Miss Nancy. I guess Sarah is
gone and her memory is slowly leaking away
while Miss Nancy is alive in Boston and somehow my insides know the difference. While I
never will forget Sarah and I know we would
have been happy had she lived, I can let her
go. Miss Nancy, though, is another thing.

Maybe I will go back to Boston and see if I
can get her to change her opinion of me. She
thinks I'm a harsh barbarian, and maybe she's
right. She has seen me kill a man, and she
knows I can't read and don't talk too good,
either. She can't think I have anything to offer
a woman, and it would be beneath her dignity
to marry up with a man like me. I would love
her better than any other man for the rest of
her life if she would only give me the chance.
I am bone-tired of being all alone.

I hear the trumpet announcing the coming
of the morning stage. From the sound, I know
it's Jess Wright who's driving. I hear them pull
up in front, and the sounds of voices as the
passengers get down. I'm not in any hurry to
go inside and put up with a passel of strangers,
especially once they find out who I am, so I stay

where I am and think on Sarah and Nancy and how my life is not going to be so much if I cannot get Nancy to share it with me.

Guess I'm feeling what James is feeling about Miss Luis, only Nancy doesn't love me back and maybe never will. *Prob'ly* never will. I believe I would be setting myself up for hurt and shame if I try to change her mind. I remember how Lilly Lipman shamed me and how bad and hateful I felt after she did. What makes me think that Nancy would treat me any different?

The back door opens and someone comes out, prob'ly to go to the necessary. The footsteps continue in my direction, however, and I loose the thong from my gun but don't turn around. Don't people know when a man wants to be alone?

The footsteps stop behind me, and I can tell they don't belong to a big person, but old Sam Colt made size not so important anymore. My hand hovers close to my gun.

"Hello, Walker," Nancy says, and my breath catches in my throat. I turn away from Sarah's grave and reach out without thinking. Like James, my life is suddenly laid out for me too, and it is good.

For sure.